# Permanently Deleted

AMY E. LILLY

Library of Congress Control Number:  2016904812

1st Edition
©2016 Amy Lilly
Bella Lilly Press
King George, VA

ISBN-13: 9780692663936 (paperback)

# DEDICATION

To all my readers who love Phee and her friends as much as I do. Thank you for sharing the journey with me.

# ACKNOWLEDGMENTS

This book could not have been possible without my family and friends and their infinite patience as I killed characters in numerous scenarios and chattered *ad nauseum* about the next chapter of the book. I sometimes forget these characters aren't real and not everyone knows their life story. A big thank you to my sister-in-law, Shari, for her amazing work on my cover. I look forward to writing the next Phee Jefferson book.

# CHAPTER ONE

I was at the circulation desk in the library checking in the large cart of books next to me. I wanted to get everything done and shelved before I went home in a few minutes. The last patron was packing up to leave when Juliet burst through the front doors.

"Phee, you've got to come," Juliet panted.

"I'm busy, Juliet," I said, stifling my exasperation at the interruption. "I need to get this done." I scanned another book.

Juliet slammed her hand down in front of me. Startled at her sudden burst of anger, I looked up and saw Juliet's eyes. "What in the world is the matter, Juls."

"It's Nellie Jo. They found Mike dead at the pickle factory," Juliet sobbed, "and Clint's arrested her. Phee, he said she killed him. Nellie killed her husband!"

I sat back and tried to process Juliet's news. Nellie arrested for murder? It had to be a mistake. Since Juliet had helped me solve Elody Campbell's murder, she saw crime everywhere she looked. Poor Mr. Crum had to walk his dog in the predawn hours to avoid Juliet's watchful gaze. She swore he didn't use a pooper scooper when he walked his Schnauzer.

"You must have heard bad information. There's no way Nellie killed Mike. Take a breath. Start at the beginning and tell me what's going on."

"Nobody has time for that!" Juliet shouted. "Nellie's in jail. Mike is dead. Grab your purse and let's go."

I held my hands up in defeat. "Give me five minutes to shut

everything down and lock up. We'll head over to the sheriff's office and talk to Clint and Lu. I'm sure it's a misunderstanding." I shut off the computer and grabbed my sweater and purse. Juliet paced in front of the exit as I flipped off all the lights and locked the doors.

"Nellie won't do well in prison. She's too sweet and trusting," Juliet blurted. "I've got two hundred dollars in savings to help with bail money. Do you think Mom and Dad will chip in?" Juliet jogged down the sidewalk towards the sheriff's.

"Wait until we find out what's going on before you break open your piggy bank," I said, huffing as my short legs struggled to catch up with Juliet's long stride.

Juliet ignored me and burst through the glass doors of the sheriff's office causing the glass to shudder in the frame. Tina looked up from where she sat flipping through a gossip magazine. "Where's Nellie? Why did you arrest her?" Juliet's eyes darted around the small front office until they lighted on Lu who had come out of her office in the back. "Lu? What the heck is going on?"

"Settle down," Lu said, holding up her hands defensively.

"Settle down? Settle down? Clint slapped cuffs on Nellie like she was a common criminal and you want me to settle down?" Juliet gave an exasperated snort of laughter.

The door to the sheriff's slammed open behind us. Valerie, Corinne Thomas and Charlie marched in. Charlie demanded to see Nellie. They all wanted to know why she was under arrest. I couldn't figure out who was saying what as everyone's voices rose in volume.

Lu leaped up on the Tina's desk and pulled out her gun. "Everybody sit down and be quiet or I'm gonna shoot!"

"No need to shoot anyone," Clint drawled as he walked into

the reception area. "Nellie isn't under arrest. I didn't cuff her. She's here to answer questions about Mike. You all need to go home and let the police do their job." He looked pointedly at Juliet and then turned his gaze towards me.

I avoided his eyes. I stepped up next to Juliet and put my arm around her shoulders. "Come on, Juls. Let the professionals," I hesitated on the word, "do their job. I'm sure Nellie will straighten everything out, and we'll have a big laugh with her tomorrow at the shop."

"I doubt Nellie will be open for business tomorrow. Mike was found dead in a vat at the pickle factory. Based on our initial investigation, it was definitely murder."

# CHAPTER TWO

There was a collective gasp from the gathered crowd. Juliet recovered first. "Clint, there's no way Nellie killed Mike."

"I didn't say she did. Anyone who came into contact with the victim over the past twenty-four hours is a person of interest and has to be questioned," Clint explained. "That includes Nellie. Everyone needs to head home. We're in the early stages of the investigation. I'm sure Sheriff Dawes will let everyone know what's going on once we have more information."

"You better treat Nellie Jo with respect or you cops will have to answer to me," Charlie said with a bravado that belied his age. "She's like family."

"That's right. Nellie's family," Corrine chimed in.

"I care about Nellie, too, folks, but we have a job to do, so let us do it," Lu said, stepping forward. She herded everyone towards the door. "The best thing you can do for her is go home and let us investigate." She held the door open and practically pushed us outside.

I gave Clint one last look before grabbing Juliet by the elbow. "Let's go. Lu's right. There's nothing we can do tonight."

"This sucks!" Juliet protested. "I can't believe your boyfriend arrested Nellie."

"She's not under arrest. You heard what he said. She's answering questions. It's typical for any murder investigation. The cops have to talk to the spouse and family."

"I can't believe Mike's been murdered."

"Me either," I said. "It's weird, but as long as they've lived here, I can't say I knew Mike very well. Nellie's like everyone's favorite aunt, but Mike…well, he was so beige next to Nellie. I can't imagine him doing anything to make someone kill him."

"I never thought about it, but you're right. He didn't associate with people in Miller's Cove. I've run into him a time or two at some town festivals, but I rarely saw him at the coffee shop."

"I guess he was busy making pickles." I heard a loud rumbling in the distance. "Is that thunder?"

"Nope. It's that." Juliet pointed to a large, black truck rolling down the street.

The truck pulled to a stop in front of us. "Is that an alligator on the hood?" I asked Juliet.

"It is." Her eyes were wide as she took in the alligator, a large snorkel on the hood and oversized tires.

"Holy tacky tacos. Who in the heck drives around Miller's Cove with a dead reptile on their vehicle?"

In answer to my question, the door of the truck opened. A mountain of a man stepped out of the truck. Alligator skin cowboy boots landed on the sidewalk. The sun glinted off the shiny silver tips. He wore a black cowboy hat, a tight, white t-shirt and even tighter blue jeans.

"Ladies, is that the sheriff's office behind you?" he asked in a Southern drawl.

"It is," Juliet said. She stepped forward and held out her hand. "Juliet. Nice to meet you."

Her hand disappeared into his hairy bear paw of a hand. "Eddie. Mike Johnson is – was my uncle."

"I'm Phee Jefferson. I knew your uncle. I'm sorry for your loss. If there is anything my sister and I can do to help, please let us know."

"I appreciate your condolences, Miss Jefferson. I'm aiming

to bag me a killer. It's open hunting season in these parts on whoever killed my uncle." He patted the small holster attached to his belt. I hadn't noticed the gun. Perhaps because my eyes were too busy being bedazzled by the large belt buckle featuring silver and gold fighting roosters.

"The police are working hard to find out what happened to Mike," Juliet said.

"Well, that may be, but I don't hold much faith in law enforcement. We got our own brand of justice where I hail from, and I'll just say it's fast and permanent. Uncle Mike was a good man and didn't deserve the end he got."

"What happened? The police wouldn't tell us much," Juliet probed. I shot her a cautioning look. I wanted to hear what Eddie had to say as much as she did, but this man was like a coiled rattler ready to strike at the nearest moving target. I didn't want to be that target.

"I just left the factory. I've been traveling back and forth between here and Louisiana the past few months learning the business. Best I can figure, two workers found Uncle Mike face down in a pickle vat. Looks like he drowned. Now what kind of grown man goes swimming in a pickle vat? None. Somebody pushed him in and held him down. When I find out who did it, I'm gonna make them pay with their life!" Eddie punched his left fist into his open palm. He spun on his heel and stalked into the sheriff's office.

"Whew! I wouldn't want to be in the killer's shoes right now. Alligator Eddie looks like he would kick butt and ask about guilt later. I wonder if he skinned the gator for those boots he was wearing," Juliet mused.

"I wonder who hated Mike enough to murder him," I said.

# CHAPTER THREE

Juliet and I headed down the sidewalk towards Odd Couple's. As we entered the diner, I was shocked to see every table was full. I eyed the diners and saw more strangers than familiar faces.

"Who are all these people? Is there something going on down at the lake? It's as packed now as it is in the summer," I said.

"It's the protesters," Juliet responded. "Mom told me about it this morning when I went over for breakfast."

"Protesters? What the heck are they protesting in Miller's Cove? Too much peace and quiet?"

"Mike Johnson's pickle factory."

"Who protests pickles?" I asked. As I looked around the dining room, I noticed that many of the diners wore t-shirts with the words "Stop the Dill Fish Kill" emblazoned across their chest. "What's up with the t-shirts."

"We're protesting Peck o' Pickles dumping brine into the stream next to the factory. It's killing the fish," a voice said from behind me.

I turned and saw Willow had come into the restaurant behind Juliet and me. She, too, wore a t-shirt protesting fish kills, but Willow's sported a fish upside down in the throes of death.

"Willow," Juliet said. "I missed you at yoga class yesterday evening."

"Sorry," Willow said. "I was at the factory protesting with the others. We've been down there all week. That factory is a menace to the environment. The spirits are not happy with Peck o' Pickles right now." Willow communed regularly with her spirit guides. She raised her hand and waved at a group of protesters already seated at a table. "I want you to meet some of the leaders of the group."

Willow wound her way through the crowded diner to a table with two earthy looking women in huarache sandals and tie-dyed shirts with fish swimming on the front. I eyed the words printed on their chests - *Don't be a Big Dill. Stop the Fish Kill.* "Darcy. Dragonfly. This is Juliet and her sister, Phee. They are righteous yoga chicks."

"Nice to meet you. I'm Darcy." She was in her mid-forties with graying brown hair and a warm smile. "I really dig Miller's Cove."

"Except for the creep that's dumping noxious crap in the creek and killing all the croakers," Darcy's companion said with a bitter edge to her voice. "I'm Dragonfly."

"This is the first I've heard about all of this," I said. "What's going on?"

"Mike Johnson, CEO and first-class jerk of Peck o' Pickles, has been killing the fish in the stream that feeds the lake. He's been dumping all of his brine from his pickle vats into the water," Dragonfly explained. "I've called the EPA and every other initialed government agency and all they say is that they'll investigate. They've got a backlog of cases. I gathered up my crew, and we headed here to set Johnson straight. So far, he's refused to meet with us and negotiate, but I'm ready to pull out the big guns. No more Miss Nice Guy for Mr. Picklepuss!"

"So you protested at the factory this weekend, too?" Juliet asked.

"Yep!" Dragonfly said. "We staged a huge blockade around the factory yesterday until a redneck in a gas-guzzling truck tried to run us over last night. Eventually, the owner has to come clean. They always do. Public image to maintain and all that crap."

"I doubt Mike will meet with you," I said.

"Darcy can be persuasive," Willow assured me. "If not, we'll use any means necessary to shut the factory down until the dumping stops."

"You don't understand," I said. "Mike won't be meeting with anyone. He's dead."

"You're joking, right?" Darcy visibly paled. "He can't be dead."

"He's dead," Juliet said. "We just came from the sheriff's office. They said it was murder."

"Oh my goddess!" Willow exclaimed. "That's horrible. I mean, the guy was a first-class loser, but nobody deserves to be murdered." Her hands fluttered nervously.

"Karma," Dragonfly said. "It's a bitch."

Darcy flashed her a dark look. "Not cool, Dragonfly. Not cool. We want to heal the world. Not wish ill upon others." She turned back to us. "We try to achieve our goals through peaceful means."

"The spirits frown on violence," Willow said, nodding her head. "I'll consult the stones and see what insight they can bring."

"Well, maybe the spirits can tell the sheriff that Nellie didn't kill her husband," I said, only half in jest. Although I wasn't a true believer, Willow seemed to have an uncanny knack for knowing what to say in times of turmoil.

"Does the sheriff have a suspect in custody?" Darcy asked.

"They brought Mike's wife, Nellie, in for questioning," Juliet said. "As if anyone as sweet as Nellie could kill anyone. I knew I should've gone to police academy. If I was a deputy, I'd be a rabid bloodhound tracking the perp. Neither rain, nor snow, nor dark of night would keep me from taking down the murderer."

"Uh…you mixed up the post office motto and the law," I laughed.

"Whatever," Juliet shrugged. "I wouldn't waste my time thinking Nellie could have done it. With the time they're wasting bothering Nellie, the real suspect is getting away."

"Clint's doing his job. He has to question everyone in Mike's life," I said a little defensively. "You're the 1970s cop show junkie. The wife is suspect number one until they question everyone. Clint will get to the bottom of it."

Juliet crossed her arms and harrumphed. A moment later, a nearby booth came open. We said goodbye to Willow and her friends and slid into our seats. Juliet and I had eaten at Odd Couple's since we were teenagers, so we didn't need menus.

"I'd like the Desi burger with fries and a root beer, please," I told Stephanie when she came to take our order.

"Same for me." After Stephanie walked away, Juliet leaned back and eyed me.

"What?"

"So what is up with you and the dashing deputy?"

"We're… good," I said. "We're both busy."

"I call baloney and macaroni. The tension between the two of you when we were at the station was noticeable to everyone. Spill it."

"I don't know what to tell you," I said. I didn't. Clint and I talked every day and occasionally went to dinner. Our relationship had turned brittle as an autumn leaf, ready to crumble at the smallest gust of wind. I wanted to move forward with our relationship, but Clint threw a monkey wrench into the works when he said he didn't want a commitment or plans for a future. Even worse, he refused to talk about it again. "I want the house, the two point five kids and ten kittens. He wants things to stay exactly as they are. I love him, but what can I do? Break up and be alone and heartbroken?"

"Phee, you deserve to get everything in life you want. If you want marriage and a family and he doesn't, then maybe he isn't the one. I mean, I love the guy, too. Clint's like family, but it doesn't give him a free pass to be a jerk. He breaka your heart. I breaka his face!" Juliet put her fists up and did a quick fake jab.

"Settle down, Muhammad Ali. It's okay. I've made peace with his decision for now."

"I don't believe you for a second, but I'll leave it alone. I'm still hotter than a baked potato that he had Nellie in the back of the cruiser like she was a hardened criminal."

"Don't get mad, Juls." I took a sip of my root beer. "Get investigating!"

# CHAPTER FOUR

After we finished eating, Juliet dropped me off at my house. I promised I would be at her butt crack o' dawn yoga class in the morning.

"Don't come crawling in halfway through the class like you did last week," Juliet warned. "I will call you out in front of everyone and make you downward dog all day. Blood is not thicker than yogi karma, Flea!"

"I won't be late," I promised. "Stop calling me Flea!"

She honked her horn as she zoomed off in her blue Karmann Ghia convertible, Ole Blue. The weather had been mild all week. I had walked to work and left my trusty VW van, Velma, parked in my driveway. Unlocking my front door, my twenty-five tons of fluffy love cat, Ferdie, twined his way between my legs mewing his pleas for food. I hurried to the kitchen before his meows turned to grumpy caterwauling.

I dumped a half can of food onto his dry kibbles. "Happy?" Ferdie, typical of his fickle cat nature, ignored me in favor of dinner.

I turned the gas on the stove to boil water for tea. I needed to sit and think about Mike's murder and Nellie. After fixing myself a cup of Moroccan mint tea, I carried it to my vintage Formica table.

"Ferdie, I have to figure out who hated Mike Johnson enough to kill him." I grabbed a pen and some paper to list the people who had a reason to kill Mike. After a minute, the list only had one name - Nellie.

"I can't leave her off the list yet. Even though Nellie wouldn't have done it, Nancy Drew would include her."

Ferdie, finished with his dinner, lifted his tail and trotted out of the room, a clear sign of what he thought about Nellie as a suspect.

I thought about Mike. He and Nellie moved to Miller's Cove from Louisiana over twenty years ago. Mike had built the pickle factory and as far as I knew, his business was successful. He sold enough pickles to buy Nellie her coffee shop five years ago. Rumor was he paid cash for the business. He and Nellie lived in a nice house on a large tract of land outside of town where they raised horses.

I didn't know Mike or his friends. Despite talking to Nellie almost daily, she never shared much information about her husband. Whenever I asked how he was doing, her standard reply was "working hard."

Putting down my pen, I headed next door to talk to Oscar. Oscar Pollack was eighty years old and had been the mayor of Miller's Cove for more years than I've been alive. He knew everything about everyone. More importantly, he loved to gossip.

Moments later, I stood knocking on his door. Oscar answered the door wrapped in a ratty red flannel robe and leather moccasin slippers on his feet. His few remaining wisps of gray hair stood in tufts all over his head.

"I'm sorry, Oscar. I didn't realize you were in bed," I apologized.

Oscar waved my apology away. "I wasn't asleep. I've been in my pajamas for the past two days fighting off a darn cold." He let out a large sneeze. He reached into his robe pocket and pulled out a tattered handkerchief. Oscar wiped his already red nose. He motioned me inside and shuffled towards his living room. I followed and sat on the couch opposite his beat-up blue recliner.

"Can I bring you anything? Soup? Tea?" I asked. His nose was swollen and his eyes were puffy.

"A bottle of whiskey wouldn't go unappreciated," Oscar said. At my shocked look, he said, "My Mary, God rest her soul, swore by whiskey with a little honey or brown sugar to fight off a cold. The woman was a teetotaler unless she had a cold. Just between you and me, she had a lot of colds."

"Well, if Mrs. Pollack swore by it, then it must have worked," I said. I rose from the couch to leave. "I wanted to ask you about Mike Johnson, but it can wait. I can come back another time when you're feeling better."

"Mike Johnson," Oscar drawled. A slight air of contempt permeated his words. "What's that slick weasel done now?"

I sat back down. "He's been murdered."

"Well, isn't that interesting?" Oscar leaned forward and fixed his puffy eyes on me. "What happened?"

I ignored the eager gleam in Oscar's eyes. "I was at the sheriff's office earlier. They brought Nellie in to question her about his death. He was found dead at the factory."

"Woo doggie. This is a kawinkydink. Couldn't happen to a better person." Oscar gave a harsh bark of laughter that ended in a coughing spasm. When his coughing subsided and he had caught his breath, he said, "Mike Johnson was a cheater. He cheated on his wife, and he cheated in his business. Guess the old expression that cheaters never prosper finally rang true."

"Mike cheated on Nellie? Who was he cheating with? Did she know?" I asked.

"Whoa. Hold on. Mike's been cheating on Nellie with a two-bit dancer from Lamplighter Lounge."

"Lamplighter Lounge?"

"It's a strip club outside of town on the way to Hawkins," Oscar explained. "I don't believe Nellie knew about his indiscretion, but who knows what goes on behind closed doors. He was catting around with some floozy named Dusty or Misty… something with a Rose. Dusty Rose. That was her name."

"It sounds like you knew more than a little bit about what went on behind closed doors," I said, only half-joking.

"I make it my business to find out things. You can't run a town or a business without knowing what people are doing. Gives you the upper hand to know what makes a person tick."

"I'll keep my curtains closed at night," I laughed uneasily. My octogenarian neighbor wasn't as sweet as I believed.

"You have nothing to worry about from me, Phee." He leaned forward and patted my knee. "I'm retired from politics and from business. I don't have a need for information like I used to. Besides, what bad deeds would a librarian commit?"

"I fold the corners of my novel's pages down sometimes."

"I rest my case." Oscar coughed hard and let out a loud sneeze. "I'd better get back in bed, and you'd better get out of here before I make you sick."

I stood up to leave. I hesitated and turned back. "Oscar, you said Mike was a cheat in business. What did you mean?"

"Nothing I could put my finger on but ask yourself this. How did Mike Johnson come up with cash to buy that factory, build an extravagant home outside of town and pay cash for Nellie Jo's Cup O' Joe? The pickle business is good, but it isn't good enough for that kind of money. Plus, there's been late night deliveries to the pickle factory lately and it's making me uneasy."

As I made my way back to my house I wondered how I could explain to my mother that I needed to go to a strip club.

# CHAPTER FIVE

I poured myself a glass of wine and settled on my chaise lounge. The revelation that Mike wasn't just a stuffy pickle pusher boggled my mind. I called Juliet. I wanted to see if she knew Mike was cheating on Nellie.

"Whatever you're selling, I'm not buying," Juliet said when she answered the phone.

"It's me."

"I know it's you. There's this modern day invention called caller identification. What's up?"

"Mike was cheating on Nellie with a stripper from the Lamplighter Lounge." The words came out in a rush. I still had a hard time believing it. I didn't believe Mike would betray Nellie.

"That dive bar? With Mike's money, he could afford a higher class of mistress," Juliet said.

"Aren't you surprised?"

"Not really. I like Nellie, but Mike gave me the heebie jeebies. It was the way he looked at me. I felt like a prize cow up for auction."

"I never got that vibe from him," I protested. "He was a gray little man who never said two words to me any time I saw him."

"He didn't need to say anything. His eyes said it all and not in the hot way they describe in the romance novels. His eyes were more front desk creepy guy at a No Tell Motel."

"Hmmm…if you say so. Oscar said he was a cheater in business and in his marriage."

"Well, if Oscar said it, then it must be true. That man has more dirt on folks in this town than a gardener."

Clearly, I was the only naïve enough to assume my neighbor was a feeble, old man. "I want to go to the Lamplighter. You need to come with me."

"When? Now?"

"Tomorrow night after I get off work."

"So you want us to go to a strip club and see if we can figure out who Mike was sleeping with?"

"Yes."

"Two girls going to a strip club on a Tuesday night," Juliet said.

"Yes."

"You don't see a problem with this plan?"

"No. What's wrong?"

"Two girls. Strip club. Dive." Juliet said. "Hell's bells, Phee. We'll stick out like snowmen at a Fourth of July celebration. Girls do not go to strip clubs on their own. Besides, Mom and Dad would kill us."

"Wade can go with us for protection. Ask him."

Juliet laughed. "I don't need to ask. Any man with a pulse wouldn't turn down a free pass from his girlfriend to go see strippers. I'll pick you up at seven, and we'll head over there. Wear something not quite so librarian." She hung up.

What did she mean by that? I had a phenomenal vintage wardrobe. The other day I'd found an amazing wrap dress à la Diane von Fürstenberg. I took a sip of wine and picked up the novel I was reading. I read all of Kathy Reich's Temperance Brennan series as soon as they were published. I couldn't wait for the next one to come out, so I was reading the first book in the series again.

I read for an hour before heading off to bed. As I slipped

into my favorite sheep in tiara pajamas, I thought about Nellie and wondered if she was still at the sheriff's office or if she was home. It had to be hard for her to return to that big empty house by herself. Even if Mike was a dirty cheating dog, Nellie always seemed head-over-heels in love with him.

The next day was busy at the library. Wade came in that afternoon for his shift, but we didn't have time to talk about my plans for the evening. Right before closing, Juliet strutted in to the library wearing four-inch spike boots that came up to her knees. A short skirt showed off her long tanned legs. A fringed t-shirt left little to the imagination and even less covering her ample assets.

Wade let out a low wolf whistle. "Hello, Hot Stuff. Come to Papa."

"Uh…yuck. Still on the clock there, mister, and you are creeping out your boss," I said. "Juliet, what in Sam Hill are you wearing and what eighties hair band groupie did you kill to get that outfit?"

"Like it?" Juliet twirled around to provide us with the full effect of her ensemble.

"I like it." Wade leered at her. "If I knew you would dress like that, I would have taken you to a dive bar a long time ago."

"Again, your boss. Right here. Grossed out that you are looking at my baby sister like a glazed lamb chop."

Juliet leaned over the circulation desk and gave Wade a kiss. "I got this t-shirt at the Harley shop in Burlington a couple of years ago. Remember the biker I was dating? He took me shopping and bought me this t-shirt. Never had a chance to wear it until now."

"I might not have a Hog, but my wheels roll all night long," Wade said, winking at Juliet as he did a wheelie in his wheelchair. He was waiting for a new suspension system for one of his prosthetic legs, so he was back in his wheelchair for the next few days.

"On that disturbing note, I'm walking away to turn everything off so we can get out of here." I left Juliet and Wade to shut down the computers and turn off the lights in the bathrooms and study rooms.

Ten minutes later, we climbed into Velma and headed towards the Lamplighter Lounge. Juliet rode shotgun.

"Any word on Nellie?" I asked. "The town grapevine says she's back home but under strict orders not to leave town."

"I heard the same thing," Juliet said. "I asked around, but the only thing anyone said is that Mike was floating in one of the big pickle vats at the factory. No word if he drowned, was shot, got whacked on the head or what. Has Clint told you anything?"

"I haven't talked to Clint. I didn't want to bother him last night. To be honest, things are so rocky between us…" I trailed off, not sure what to say.

"Clint's a good guy, Phee," Wade said. "Guys never act like we have feelings or anything remotely sensitive. He cares about you. Clint has some kind of bad juju going on in his head right now. I understand what it's like to live inside your head too much."

"Change of subject before Phee turns into the Doom and Gloom Queen. With that black silk blouse and black jeans, she is one step away from being there already."

"I had to wear something that transitioned from work to strip club without screaming floozy. I look classy, not trashy," I protested. I'd left my hair down and had on a pair of low-heeled ankle boots.

"You should have added some color. Black washes you out, but at least your outfit doesn't scream librarian. Give me your overdue books or else!"

"Ha ha. Where do I need to turn?" I squinted as I tried to read the faded road signs as we left the town limits of Miller's Cove and headed towards Hawkins. The road signs in the county sported graffiti if they existed at all.

"Up here." Juliet pointed. "Take the next right and the Lamplighter Lounge should be about a half mile up on the left."

A minute later, I pulled Velma into the parking lot next to a windowless box-shaped building with a neon dancing naked woman with a lamp in her hand.

"Here goes nothing. Remember what happens at the strip club, stays in the strip club," Juliet joked.

"Nothing will happen in the strip club except for checking out the home wrecking hussy, Dusty Rose," I said.

"I brought dollar bills," Wade piped in as he slid himself into his wheelchair. Juliet chucked him gently on the back of his head. "Hey! It's part of my cover!"

We headed into the bar. The relative quiet of the parking lot gave way to loud music and pulsing lights. A spotlight focused on the stage where a bleached blonde strutted around a pole in high heels and not much else.

"Let's go ask the bartender about Dusty," I said and made my way to the scarred wooden bar. The bartender was lazily wiping glasses with a dirty rag that may have been white in a previous century.

"What can I getcha?"

"I'm looking for someone. Dusty Rose? Is she here tonight?" I asked.

"Yep."

"Can you point her out? I need to talk to her."

"Nope."

"Why not?" My hands touched the sticky bar top. I grimaced and wiped them on my jeans.

"You want to talk to my girls, then you need to buy a drink. We gotta two drink minimum."

"I'll take a diet soda," I said trying to keep the irritation from my voice.

"What about them?" He nodded towards Juliet and Wade.

"I'll take a Corona with a lime," Juliet said.

"We got Bud, Bud Light and Miller Lite on tap. Ain't got no Corona." He set down the glass. He took the dirty rag and wiped the bar in front of me.

"A gin and tonic then," Juliet said. She looked at me and arched an eyebrow.

"I'll take a Bud," Wade said and pulled out his wallet to pay. He laid a twenty on the bar. "Now how about pointing us towards Dusty?"

"She's in back, but she'll be coming out in a little while to dance."

"Thanks." Wade took his beer and his change. He tossed a dollar bill on the bar for a tip and wheeled towards a table near the stage.

"Do we need to get this close to the action?" I hissed. My eyes darted around taking the slack-jawed audience.

"When she leans down to let me tuck a dollar into her G-string, I'll ask her to come talk to us after her dance," Wade explained.

"Good thing you brought plenty of dollar bills," Juliet said. Despite the nonchalance in her voice, I noticed she laid a possessive hand on his shoulder.

We sat at a relatively clean table. I didn't even want to consider what lived on the chairs. There wasn't enough hand sanitizer in the world to make me feel less dirty. My boots stuck to the floor and the smell of beer and body odor made me gag.

The girl on stage finished her dance with a split to the ground and then sashayed off stage. A few beats later, the music morphed into Warrant's *Cherry Pie* and an attractive busty blonde strutted on stage in platform heels, grabbed the pole in the center of the stage, and danced.

"That's got to be Dusty Rose," Juliet said.

"How do you know?" I asked. I didn't want to stare at the dancing woman too long in case she expected me to tuck money into her G-string.

"She has a rose tattooed on her derriere," Wade pointed out.

"I'd call that a clue," Juliet said. "My sleuthing skills are top-notch."

"See if you can get her attention, Wade," I said. "We need to see what she knows about Mike and his murder."

Wade rolled closer to the stage and waved a five dollar bill at the dancer. He gave her a wide smile and winked. A few beats of the music later, she leaned down and shimmied at him. He tucked the bill into her ample cleavage and said a few words to her that were drowned out by the loud music. She nodded and sashayed back to the dance pole.

Wade steered his chair back to the table and picked up his beer. "Mission complete. I asked her to come to our table after her dance. I offered her fifty bucks."

"Fifty dollars! That's a little rich for this cockroach cocktail joint!" Juliet exclaimed. "You'd better be glad I'm a strong, confident woman who knows fifty ways to kill you in your sleep because you were acting a little too friendly with Miss Dusty Rose."

"I should get combat pay for this duty. A nice, wholesome guy like myself being forced to come to a bar with two gorgeous women and watch other women strip. You'll need to pay for my therapy for years. Your mother would be shocked at how you two have corrupted me." He put an arm around Juliet and kissed her. "Sugar booger, you know I only want you."

Juliet giggled and kissed him back. "I know that. I was making sure you knew it."

"Someone find me a pair of galoshes because it's getting deep in here," I said. I loved Juliet and Wade together. They were comfortably in love with each other. I wished Clint and I had that easy flow of emotion. Lately, we were like two stranger cats who were fighting out their boundaries.

"Earth to Flea. Come in, Flea." Juliet waved a hand in front of my face. "Dusty's routine is over. Are you with us?"

"Yes. Sorry. I was thinking about…things."

Dusty slid into the seat next to Wade. She caught the bartender's attention and shouted, "Bring me a whiskey and soda, Bruce." Turning back to us, she asked, "So what's up? You two don't look like the type of girls that go to strip clubs."

"We came to talk to you about Mike," Juliet said.

"Mike? I'm not sure I know a Mike. I know a Matt, but no Mike." Her eyes slid furtively away from Juliet's. Bruce plopped her drink down in front of her. She took a sip and said, "I wish I could help you out, but I think you've got the wrong person."

I didn't believe her for a minute. "That's too bad. We had some news about Mike Johnson we needed to tell you, but if you don't know him…"

"Hold on a second. I don't think I do. The name sounds familiar, but I meet a lot of guys in my line of work." She took another sip of her drink. "What's the news? I mean, if it's not too personal."

"Mike was found dead Monday morning," Juliet said.

Dusty was silent for a moment. She dropped her face into her hands and began to cry. "I lied. I know Mike. He's my…he was my boyfriend. I thought his wife sent you to threaten me again." Mascara tears tracked a crooked line down her cheeks.

"I'm sorry. Did you say Mike's wife threatened you?" Juliet asked. "When was this?"

Dusty sniffled and wiped her nose with the back of her hand. "Saturday night. She climbed up on the stage and screamed at me right in the middle of my routine. She was crazy mad."

"Did you know he was married? I mean, you can't blame Nellie for being angry. You were having an affair with her husband," I said. I hope this woman didn't expect us to feel sorry for her.

"Not at first, but I figured it out soon enough. By the time I did, I was in love." She shrugged her shoulders. "A girl wants what a girl wants. Now he's gone." She dropped her face into her hands.

"Waz going on here?" A large man with a faded green t-shirt that failed to cover his ample belly stumbled his way to our table. "Why…why you crying, Dusty? These folks botherin' you?" He swayed back and forth.

"Hey, buddy, we're having a private conversation with Dusty," Wade said. "You can talk to her in a few minutes."

"Do I know you?" He squinted at Wade and tried to focus. "I'm a friend of Dusty's and you're making her cry, buddy." He poked at Wade with his sausage fingers. Somehow he managed to push the wheelchair and lost his balance. He stumbled, caught himself and stumbled backwards against me. The drunk tried to steady himself by grabbing my chair but grabbed my chest instead.

"Get your grubby paws off of me!" I yelled.

He gave me a sloppy grin which showed his missing front teeth. "No need to get angry, baby doll. Why don't you give me a lap dance, and I'll forgive you for makin' my friend cry?" He hiccupped and squeezed.

"Why don't you go take a flying leap off a short cliff! And get your hand off my boob!" I picked up my purse and swung it hard. It hit the drunk on the side of the head. He dropped to the ground like a sack of potatoes.

"You killed Daryl! Bruce! Call the police! She killed Daryl!" Dusty screamed. "She killed Mike and now she's killed Daryl! Police!"

"What? No! Wait! I didn't kill anybody!" I jumped up to leave.

"You aren't going anywhere," Bruce said. The skull tattoo on his arm seemed to threaten me as he flexed his biceps. "Sit down. The law's coming."

# CHAPTER SIX

Fifteen minutes later, Clint and Lu walked into the bar. I cringed and sunk down into my chair. Juliet, however, waved at them and motioned them over.

"Lu and Clint. What brings you to this fine establishment?" Juliet asked. She turned her big blue eyes heavenward. If I didn't know better, I would have sworn she was as innocent as a newborn puppy. She was like baby Cujo, but fluffy.

"Cut the crap, Juls," Clint said. "We had a call that two women and a man in a wheelchair assaulted a man. Imagine my surprise when the description that came across the radio sounded exactly like my girlfriend." He turned to me. "Phee, what the hell are you doing in this dive, and why are you assaulting people?"

Daryl was sitting at the bar and had a grungy bar towel filled with ice on his head. When he realized the law had arrived, he stumbled his way over to us. "Occifer. I want you to arres…arrest this woman for assaultin' me." He hiccupped and sat down.

"It wasn't assault!" I protested. "It was self-defense. He grabbed the girls and wouldn't let go! I only hit him with my bag to make him go away. He was so drunk it knocked him over."

Clint hefted my bag. He flipped it open and pulled out two books. Two thick hardcover books. Oops. He clicked the mike on his shoulder. "Tina, Officer Gifford and I are on scene. Looks like we got an armed and dangerous librarian. Her books are deadly."

"Roger that. Tell Phee I said hi," Tina responded back.

"I didn't mean to hurt him." I crossed my arms and glared at Clint. "He pushed Wade and wouldn't let go of my chest."

"Calm down. I believe you, Phee. What I want to know is why you and your sister are here in the first place?"

"We're here to talk to her," Juliet answered and pointed to Dusty Rose who was by the bar being comforted by another dancer.

"Who's she?" Lu asked. "Got a couple of overdue library books?"

"She," Juliet said, "is Mike's mistress. She probably killed him, too." She gave Lu a satisfied smile and waited.

"Says who?" Lu asked. "What makes you think she killed Mike?"

"Well, she clearly has motive. She's the mistress, and we all know Mike would never leave Nellie. In a fit of rage, she pushed him into the pickle vat. Pow! Bob's your uncle and Mike's dead."

"Got this all figured out, do you? Mike didn't simply drown. He had a several gashes on the back of his head, and somehow he ended up in the vat. Do you know how tall those vats are? You'd have to be fairly strong to put a grown man in one," Lu said.

"Pole dancers are in good shape," Juliet said. "They have to slide up and down a pole and that builds arm muscles."

"Really?" Lu said dryly. "You know this how?"

"They have workout classes based on pole dancer routines. I went to one when I was at a yoga conference. It's all the rage right now."

"We'll want to talk to her," Clint said. "What's her name?"

"Dusty Rose. She acted like she didn't know Mike was dead, but I don't believe her. Her tears seemed a little fake to me," I said.

"It would have been nice if you'd let us handle the investigation. We like to see a suspect's reaction when we first tell them the news in a suspicious death."

"Aha! So you admit she's a suspect!" Juliet crowed.

"No. She is a person of interest. Just like Nellie and anyone else who was close to Mike," Clint said. "Wade, can you take the girls home now and try to keep them out of trouble for a day or two?"

"Sure, but that's a full-time job, and I don't get combat pay." Wade chuckled at his own joke and grabbed Juliet's hand. "Come on, babe. Let's get home before they arrest us."

"What about her?" Daryl asked as he tried to stand up and failed. "You gonna arrest her before she kills somebody?"

"I could arrest you for drunk and disorderly. You sure you want to pursue this?" Clint placed his hand on his gun.

"No. Guess not. She's a…" Daryl struggled to come up with an appropriate insult.

"Careful, buddy, or I'll slap the cuffs on you and take you to jail. Bruce, find a ride for our friend here," Clint called over to the bartender.

I picked up my purse to follow Wade and Juliet out of the bar. Clint grabbed my arm. "Phee, I'm asking you to stay out of this investigation. There's more going on here than meets the eye."

"Is Nellie still a suspect?"

He hesitated a moment. "Yes."

"Then I'm not staying out of it until I prove to you she's innocent." I tugged my arm from his grasp.

"Phee…"

"I'm a grown woman, Clint. You can't wrap me up in cotton and only take me out when it suits you."

"Phee, now's not the time or place for that conversation."

He was right. I turned and walked out of the bar without saying a word.

# CHAPTER SEVEN

I started Velma and headed back to Miller's Cove. The silence in the van settled like a thick fog blanketing us all.

"Phee," Juliet said in a tentative voice. "You want to talk about it?"

"What's there to talk about?" I said bitterly. "One minute Clint is Mr. I Don't Want a Commitment, and the next he comes off like Mr. I Own This Woman. Men!" I slammed the steering wheel with my fist. Velma's horn gave a bleat of protest.

"He's worries about you, Phee," Wade said. "He wants you to be safe."

"Don't you dare take his side! Take these here little women home and lock them in a broom closet," I mimicked Clint's deep baritone voice. "The nerve! Well, this little woman has had enough of his games."

"Huzzah!" Juliet cheered. "Go Phee! Go Phee! It's your birthday! It's your birthday!"

I gave Juls a dirty look, but a second later, I burst into laughter. "Glad to know I have at least one cheerleader on my team. I know you two think I'm an emotional mess when it comes to Clint, but I love him. I really do. The problem is I don't want to always wonder how he feels about me. If he can't trust me enough to talk to me about what's going on inside of his head, then I can't trust him not to break my heart."

"I'm glad you're finally opening your eyes and not worshiping the ground Clint walks upon," Juliet said. "I love Clint like a brother, but you've always been blind when it comes to him. If you are going to be with him, take off the rose-colored glasses and be with him, warts and all."

"It's getting a little too *Steel Magnolias* for me," Wade interrupted. "Can we talk about beer and football or something other than chick stuff? I'm starting to feel like I need tissues and a glass of pink zinfandel."

"Poor baby." Juliet turned around to face Wade. "Is it time to take away your man card?"

"It will be if you womenfolk keep talking mushy stuff," Wade joked. "I need to get you home and lock you up in the broom closet. Remember?"

"Only if you go in there with me, Sugar Booger."

"Since you asked so nicely, Honey Buns."

"I'm going to take away your man card if you call my sister Honey Buns again!" I exclaimed.

I stopped Velma in front of Wade and Juliet's house. Juliet had finally agreed to move in with Wade last month after much wailing and gnashing of teeth. Mostly on Wade's part because Juliet wanted to transform his man cave into a karmic love nest. They finally agreed that she could change all of the bedrooms to suit her as long as she left the garage and living room alone. I pulled away after making sure they both were inside. A few minutes later, I was home and placating a noisy Ferdinand.

"What's the matter, Ferdie?" I asked him, stroking his fluffy head. Ferdie continued to meow loudly and trot back and forth in front of my back door. "Is there a mouse in the backyard?"

Ferdie gave me a disdainful look and yowled. He stretched up on his hind paws and batted at the door handle. I flipped on the outside light and peered through my kitchen door. I spotted a small form curled up on my wicker chair. Was it a cat? A raccoon? I opened the door and stepped outside. The small creature raised its head and looked at me. Under dirty matted fur, two brown eyes peered up at me.

"Hi there, little fella," I murmured softly and moved towards it. "How did you end up in my backyard?"

He wagged his tail and struggled to sit up. I held out my hand and allowed the little dog to sniff my hand. He gave me a friendly lick and whimpered. "You want to come inside, sweetheart? I've got some leftover chicken you might like." I reached down and gently picked him up. I could feel the dog's ribs under my hands and despite the warm weather, he trembled. I stroked his dirty head and brought him inside.

I put him down on the rug by the door and pulled the leftover chicken out of my refrigerator. I quickly shredded the meat from the leg bone and put it in a bowl. The little dog sniffed it, then seconds later he was licking the bowl clean. "Want some more?"

I placed another batch of shredded chicken in the bowl in front of him and added a second bowl filled with water. I patted him on his head as he ate and felt for a collar. No collar. Based on his thin body and badly matted fur, the dog had been without an owner for some time. "What should I call you? Charlie? Champ? Ruckus?"

The dog had settled down on the rug. He cocked his head and stared at me as I tried various names. "How about Fritz? You look like a Fritz." The little dog licked my hand as I scratched under his chin. "I'll have to give you a bath if you're going to stay here, but for tonight, I think we've both been through enough."

As if Fritz understood, he turned around two times and settled his small frame onto the rug. Ferdie came from his observation spot underneath the kitchen table and sniffed. Fritz opened one eye and deciding he wasn't worth the effort, closed it again. "Great job, Ferdie. I saved a little piece of chicken just for you. Who knew I had a superhero cat living under my roof." I held the piece of chicken in my hand until Ferdie daintily took it between his teeth and ate it.

I put the food back in the refrigerator and cleaned the counter. I glanced at the clock on my stove and realized it was almost midnight. Stifling a yawn, I turned off the lights and headed to bed. I guess I wouldn't be hearing from Clint. He must not be that worried about his little woman after all.

# CHAPTER EIGHT

A heavy weight on my chest startled me awake. Sunlight streamed through my windows, and I realized I hadn't set my alarm the night before. Shoving the twenty-five pound Ferdie off of me, I scrambled out of bed. "Crud! I'm going to be late for work!" I grabbed my cell phone and dialed Wade's number. "Wade. It's Phee. I overslept, so I'll be a few minutes late this morning."

"For what?" Wade asked.

"For work," I snapped. I was trying to tug pants on one-handed and wasn't in the mood for jokes. Then it hit me. "It's Wednesday, isn't it?"

"All day long, boss," Wade chuckled. "You forgot you were working Saturday, didn't you?"

"Yep," I said. "Tell Juls I'm sorry I missed yoga. I had a late night visitor last night who ended up staying the night."

"Too much information there, boss lady," Wade said.

"It's a dog. I've named him Fritz. I guess since I'm off I'll see if I can get him into the vet's office and a groomer. His fur is in need of some TLC."

"Cool. Juliet and I will stop by this evening to meet the newest addition to the Jefferson family. I've got to go unlock the doors and let my adoring fans into the library. Talk to you later."

"Bye." I tossed my cell phone onto my bed and went in search of a much-needed cup of coffee.

In the kitchen, I found Fritz still curled up on the rug by the back door. Hearing me, he lifted his head and wagged his tail. "You want to go outside, Fritz?"

I opened the back door and stood on the porch while he walked around and sniffed every bush and tree in the backyard. Overnight, the weather had cooled and a fall breeze flitted through the trees. Calling the dog back inside, I made a pot of coffee in my vintage percolator. While I waited for it, I fixed some more leftover chicken for Fritz and gave Ferdie his breakfast.

A knock interrupted my breakfast preparations. I wiped my hands on a bright blue dish towel and went to open the door. Peering through my glass side windows, I saw Nellie standing on my front porch. I hurried to unlock the door and ushered her inside.

As soon as I closed the door behind her, I gave her a hug. "I am so sorry about Mike, Nellie. I know how much you loved him."

Nellie sniffled. Her eyes were puffy and red. She looked as if she hadn't slept in days. "I sure did. I thought he loved me, too." She burst into tears.

"Come into the kitchen and sit down." I led her down the hallway and settled her into one of the kitchen chairs. I poured two cups of coffee and sat down next to her. "Tell me what's going on, Nellie? How can I help?"

"I don't think anyone can help me. I'm in a heap of trouble, Phee."

"You didn't kill Mike, did you?" I never thought this woman with her granny glasses and sweet disposition could hurt anyone, but I'd been fooled before and it almost got me killed. Had I made a mistake letting Nellie into my home?

"No. I loved his sorry tail even though he didn't deserve it. The police suspect that I killed him though. If you don't help me figure out who actually did, I might spend the rest of my life in prison." This sent her into a fresh bout of tears.

"I'll help you, Nellie, but you've got to tell me everything."

"Alright." Nellie sniffled. "Mike and me had a big knock down drag out fight on Saturday. Turns out he'd been stepping out on me and our marriage."

"With a dancer from The Lamplighter?"

"Yeah. Did everyone know he was cheating on me? Probably all laughing at me behind my back." She wiped at her eyes with an angry jerk.

"No, I don't think people knew. Even if they did, no one would laugh at you. We all love you." I reached out and patted her hand. "I found out about Dusty Rose from Oscar. Turns out he's not a huge fan of Mike's."

"Well, that's not surprising. Oscar always knows everything about everyone. It's how he kept people in line while he was in office."

"How did you find out?" I asked her.

"That dumb jackrabbit paid for her boob job with the business checking account. I'd gotten a call from our accountant who needed some information for our quarterly taxes. Imagine my surprise when I saw a receipt for breast implants." She puffed out her chest. "Look at me. Flat as a pancake. I certainly didn't have my girls enhanced to look like a Barbie doll."

"Oh no. I'm so sorry you had to find out that way. What did Mike say when you asked him about it?"

"At first he tried to deny it and say he must have gotten it by mistake or some type of cockamamie bull. I told him if he didn't come clean and tell me everything that I would drag him to court and take every dime he had ever made or ever thought of making. Of course, the fact that I threw a cast iron skillet at him and threatened to smash all of his mother's ugly china helped to motivate him to come clean. He still kept telling me it was a huge misunderstanding. He said he was going to fix things and make it right."

"That's what you were fighting about. People overheard you two yelling at the coffee shop. It's probably why the police think you had motive to kill Mike."

"They're right. I did want to kill him. I wasted thirty years of my life on that weasel rat bastard. The problem is that I didn't kill him, and you've got to help me prove it!"

# CHAPTER NINE

I told Nellie about our trip to meet Dusty Rose the previous evening. "She acted like she didn't know he was dead."

"Well, I wouldn't believe anything that came out of that scarlet hussy's mouth!" Nellie spat. "I went down there and tried to kick her skinny hind end. She kept squealing that it was all a big misunderstanding."

"Do you know how long Mike had been seeing her?" I asked as I poured us both another cup of coffee. I splashed a healthy dollop of cream into mine.

"Far as I can tell from going through all our bank accounts, a few months. I always let him handle the money. Never looked at our bank statements. He handled the books for the coffee shop and the pickle factory. Now I've got to learn how to do all of it." She took a big gulp of coffee and grimaced. "I'm a fool is what I am. A big dumb bunny no better than that harlot he was humping."

"You're not a fool, Nellie!" I protested. "You're one of the kindest women I know. I wouldn't have believed it of Mike if I hadn't talked to Dusty myself."

"Can you help prove it wasn't me?" Nellie asked.

"I'll do what I can. Tell me everything you did Sunday evening."

"Well, there might be a teeny problem with where I was Sunday," Nellie said slowly. "I was at the pickle factory spying on Mike."

"Oh, no!"

"Yep. Just like I suspected, along comes Miss Hot Pants roaring up in a red Trans Am like she owned the place. I saw her go into the factory. It must have been their trysting spot. I always thought he had a couch in his office in case he had to work late and was too tired to drive home. Guess he found better uses for it than sleeping." Nellie gave a bitter bark of laughter.

"Did you go inside the factory?"

"No. Like I told the deputies, I was so steaming mad I went home and started looking up divorce attorneys. I tore the house apart looking for all of our money and stuff related to the businesses so I could clean his clock."

"Did anybody see you at the house Sunday night?"

"No. How could they? We're a mile from our closest neighbor."

"Did you talk to anyone on the phone? Anything that might prove you were at home?" I asked. Things weren't looking good for Nellie if no one could provide her with an alibi.

"I talked to Little Ed. That's right. I did talk to someone. He called me around nine o'clock and asked me to tell Mike he was sorry he hadn't made it to the factory that day and he would see him Monday morning."

"That's a start. There'll be a record of the phone call. I'm sure the police will talk to Ed."

"They already have. Bad thing is, unless they can tell exactly when Mike died, I could still be a suspect. They said he died sometime Sunday evening."

"Crud biscuits! Did you watch television? Send any emails?"

"I don't email. Shoot! I'm lucky I can even use my stupid Smart phone. Mike got it for me. It's got so many bells and whistles on it, it makes my head hurt."

"Did Mike have any enemies?" I asked.

"Well, those hippie women outside the factory sure didn't like him. Some woman named Dragonbreath or Dragon something threatened to run him over with her Prius."

"Dragonfly. I met Darcy and her at the diner Monday. Was it true Mike was dumping brine into the stream causing a fish kill?"

"Up until now, I would have said no way would he have done something like that. Why that man loved fishing and hunting almost as much as he loved pickles. He always said going out on the lake in his boat to fish was as close to heaven on earth as he could get.

"I did hear he was a big fisherman," I said. What could have caused Mike to change so much that he went from a lover of fish and the great outdoors to enemy number one with the environmentalists? Could Dusty Rose have anything to do with his change of heart? "I need to talk to the protesters."

"I better get back home and go through more of our financial records. And I better contact an attorney. I need to find someone who can defend me if I do get charged with murder." Nellie stood up to leave. I followed her to the door. She turned and said, "Phee, thanks for believing me. I don't know if I would have been as quick to trust if the roles were reversed."

"Nellie, I'll get to the bottom of this and help clear your name. You go home and get some rest."

I shut the door behind her and leaned against it. I needed to talk to Darcy and Dragonfly again. But first, I needed to take Fritz to the vet and get him checked over.

An hour later, I was at Paws-n-Claws Veterinary Clinic. My parents had been taking our Irish Setter, Hamlet, here for years and Dr. Vicki Betters had squeezed Fritz into her busy schedule.

Dr. Betters ran her hands over Fritz's shaggy frame. She checked his ears and teeth and listened to his heart. "He appears to be about six months old. I'd guess he was a mix between a Jack Russell and a long-haired Dachshund. He's malnourished, but otherwise, he's in good health. I'd definitely take him to a groomer to get these mats cut and for a good bath. Are you planning to keep him?"

"I think Ferdinand would never forgive me if I didn't. He meowed up a storm until I went outside and found him."

"He's found his forever home," Dr. Better said and smiled. "I'll give him his first round of shots and a dewormer. You'll need to bring him back in a few weeks for the second round of shots and a weight check, but I think he'll be fine."

Half an hour later, Fritz and I were back in Velma and heading downtown. I had a bag of expensive dog food to help him put on weight, and he had a bone between his paws. The girls in the front office at the vet's had insisted he needed a treat for being so brave when he got his shots. I pulled into a parking spot in front of Tinted Love Beauty Salon. Kimmie and Kristin were the owners of the beauty and dog grooming salon. Since they were the only place in town that cut hair besides the barber shop, most people didn't mind that they did dogs' hair in the back of the shop.

Madonna's *Papa Don't Preach* blared in the shop. Kimmie, the older sister, sat on a salon chair reading a gossip magazine. She hopped up when she saw me. Her short hair was shaved on one side and sported a bright shade of magenta on the remaining long lock that fell over her left eye.

"What's up, Phee? Who's this little guy?" Kimmie asked.

"This is Fritz. I rescued him. Dr. Betters checked him over, and she suggested I have a professional cut out all the mats.

Can you fit him in on your schedule today?"

"Sure can, baby doll. Come here, Fritzie Witzie. Give Auntie Kimmie some sugar." Kimmie took Fritz's leash and picked him up. "I'll have him looking like a *GQ* dog model in about thirty minutes. You want to wait? Kristin's finishing up a manicure, so she can do something about those caterpillars you have growing over your eyeballs."

My hand went to my eyebrows. "What's wrong with my eyebrows?"

"Darling, Brooke Shields is so yesterday with the brows. You need some shaping and some thinning. Kristin will hook you up."

"Papa, don't preach! I'm in trouble deep! Papa, don't preach…tra la I don't know the rest of the words…la la la la la," Kristin caterwauled. The woman whose nails she was polishing grimaced at the off key singing.

"Who's that?" I asked Kimmie. I hadn't seen the woman in town before, and she didn't look like one of the protesters.

"Her name is Elizabeth Shields and she is with the feds," Kimmie hissed. "The FBI feds. She's here investigating some kind of financial hinky dinky going on with some business. I only know because my cousin Grace works at the hotel where she's staying. FYI, she knows your man, Clint. Rumor has it they were eating dinner together the other night. Everything alright between you two?"

"We're fine. It was probably business."

Kimmie gave me a doubtful look. Heck. The words didn't even ring true to my own ears. Clint did say he didn't want a commitment. Guess he was making sure I believed him. Kimmie gestured for me to take a seat and carried Fritz to the back of the salon. A few minutes later, Kristin put the nail dryer over the agent's hands and motioned me to a chair.

"What's up, girl? Kimmie wasn't kidding when she said those brows could use some love. Not tainted love either!" Kristin let out a loud guffaw of laughter at her own joke. Where her older sister was all eighties glam, Kristin was 1950s rockabilly. Both girls, however, loved karaoke and a good time. Their vast knowledge of song lyrics never ceased to amaze me.

"I guess I haven't been loving my brows. Who knew they were so needy?" I sat down and closed my eyes as she cleaned the area on my brow bone.

"How's Clint? I bet he's busy with this latest murder. I heard they were holding Nellie Jo as a suspect." Kristin applied wax to one brow and seconds later, she ripped off the muslin causing me to jump out of my seat.

"Nellie has to be questioned since she's his wife. Clint and I are good. Both of us have been busy with work and stuff," I said nonchalantly.

Kristin applied wax to the other brow. A second later, I felt her arm jostle against me as she went to yank the second strip of muslin. "Oh crap! Oh crap!"

I opened my eyes. "What? What's wrong?"

"I am so sorry," Elizabeth Shields said. "I'm such a clumsy person." She shrugged and gave me a sheepish smile.

"Phee, don't look. I can fix it," Kristin squeaked. "I can." She pressed the muslin back against my brow and frantically patted it.

"Fix what?" I asked. I turned my chair to look into the mirror. I had a unibrow. As in, one eyebrow over one eye. No eyebrow over the other. "Oh my sweet pepper of paella! My eyebrow is gone!"

"It's my fault. I was looking down at my nails and accidentally bumped Kristin. I really am sorry," Elizabeth apologized again. If she was so sorry, why did she have a triumphant gleam to her eyes?

"It's okay. I'm sure Kristin will fix it," I said smoothly. No way was I going to let this polished blonde federal agent know that inside my voice was screaming *Eyebrow Cyclops!*

"Your Clint's friend, Phee, aren't you? I'm Elizabeth Shields. He told me about you," Elizabeth said. "I've got to run. I'll buy you a cup of coffee next time I run into you to make up for this." She strolled out the shop door.

"That little…!" Kristin fumed. "Phee, I swear she did it on purpose. There's more than enough room for her to walk past me. I'll fix it though."

"How?" I said. "I look like a…a freak!" I wanted to cry, but I knew if I did, Kristin would fall apart. It wasn't her fault.

"I'll give you bangs!" Kristin said. "Yeah! That's what I'll do. I'll give you long bangs that you can wear swooped down over one eye to hide the missing eyebrow until it grows back."

"Like Veronica Lake?" I said with a small hint of hope that I wouldn't be a social pariah for the next six weeks.

"I don't know who that is, but sure." Kristin pulled out her scissors and began to cut on my hair. A few minutes later, she twirled my chair around to show me my new hairdo. She had managed to get my unruly red hair to fall into a natural looking swoop over my left eye. Although it didn't hide the missing eyebrow entirely, it did make it a little less noticeable.

"I can live with it," I said. "Worse comes to worst, I'll hide in a dark room for the next month."

"I am so sorry, Phee. I swear she bumped me on purpose. You can use a pencil to try to draw an eyebrow on if you think it will help. "

"I believe you. Somehow I think Miss Elizabeth Shields, federal agent, was trying to intimidate me. Well, Ophelia Jefferson is nobody's doormat!"

Fritz barked in support as Kimmie brought him out from the back room. His matted fur was gone and was now a clean, spiky light brown. He panted happily when he saw me.

"Fritz, my friend, let's go solve a murder and kick some FBI behind!"

# CHAPTER TEN

I decided to let Fritz learn to socialize since we were already out. Besides, I wanted to see if I could run into Darcy and Dragonfly to ask them a few more questions. He walked along with a jaunty lift of his shaggy tail. He paused at every fire hydrant. As I neared the hardware store at the end of the block, I saw a Prius with numerous bumper stickers protesting or in support of various causes. This must be Dragonfly's Prius. I looked inside the window of the store and saw Dragonfly, Darcy and a red-haired woman at the checkout counter. I waited for them by the car.

"Darcy? Remember me? Willow's friend, Phee? I wanted to ask you a few questions about the pickle factory."

"Phee. Yes, I remember you. You're the town librarian, right?" Darcy said. She wore a paisley shirt with a beaded fringe around the neckline. She smelled strongly of patchouli and something earthy.

"That's me. Purveyor of books and knower of facts," I joked. "I wanted to ask you about the fish kill."

"More like a fishpocolypse," the red-haired girl interjected. "I'm Moonflower. Dude killed all sorts of fish. It'll take years before the stream and lake are okay."

"Really? How long has the factory been dumping brine into the water?" I asked.

"At least a month or more," Dragonfly said. "Of course, Mike Johnson swore he wasn't dumping anything into the streams, but the scores of dead trout tell a different story."

"Did you talk to Mike?" I asked.

"Darcy did. She talked to him on Sunday. What was it he said, Darcy?"

"He claimed that he had no idea how his factory came to be leaking into the stream. He swore he loved fish and would look into it," Darcy said. "It's all a bunch of hooey. All those big manufacturers claim they didn't know it was happening when we all know the bigwigs give the orders."

"You talked to him on Sunday?" I asked. "What time?"

"I'm not sure. It was getting dark though because we were packing up to head back to the hotel," Darcy said.

"Was anyone else there?"

"I saw some kind of sports car. I think it was red or burgundy. I didn't see anyone though."

So Dusty Rose was at the factory when Darcy was there. Clearly, Dusty Rose had the opportunity to kill Mike if she was there that evening.

"Did Mike act upset or angry that you accused him of killing the fish?"

"That's what was weird. He got quiet and he looked upset, but not at me. He got kind of pushy then and ordered me to leave his factory."

"Dude copped an attitude," Moonflower growled. "We are the earth keepers. If we don't take care of what the goddess has given us, who will?"

I thanked the women for their time and headed back to Velma. Time to go home and think about what I had learned.

I was halfway home when Velma sputtered and rolled to a stop in the middle of Lemon Street. I tried to start her again and she gave a weak, half-hearted whir and died.

"Great! Just great!" I scowled. I patted Fritz and told him to stay put in his seat. I walked around to the rear of Velma where her engine was and lifted the lid to see what was going on with my trusty ride. I looked at the tangled mess of wires and hoses and realized I had absolutely no idea what I was looking at. Perhaps I should have taken auto shop in high school as an elective rather than choir. I jiggled a couple of wires and hopped back into the driver's seat to try to start her. This time, Velma let out a clicking noise and then nothing.

I laid my head on the steering wheel. "Why me? One eyebrow. Boyfriend is a Neanderthal. Now my ride or die van is giving up." I heaved a sigh. Fritz whined and licked my hand. "It's alright, boy. At least now you have a warm, safe house and much better hair than you did when I met you."

Someone tapped on my window. I looked and saw Anthony Ziegfried. I rolled down my window. "Anthony! What are you doing here?"

"I'm here for a much needed and deserved break from the campaign trail. I was on my way to see if you were home since you weren't at the library when I stopped by earlier. Car troubles?"

"How'd you know?" I asked. Anthony had saved my life and helped catch two murderers this past summer. He worked for Senator Campbell.

"The fact that you are stopped in the middle of the road and talking to yourself was a small clue. I'm getting pretty good at solving mysteries." He grinned at me.

"I was talking to my dog, Fritz, thank you very much," I said with a haughty lift of my nose. "Oh! Does that make it even worse?" I laughed at the idea that talking to a dog might be better than talking to myself.

"I talk to myself and to animals all the time," Anthony said. "I just don't do it while stopped in the middle of a street."

"Velma died on me and I can't get her started. She's making a horrible clicking noise."

"Sounds like either your battery or the alternator. Put her in neutral and I'll push you out of the middle of the road."

"I can't ask you to do that. I'll call a tow truck. I'm sure it will only take them a few minutes to get here," I protested.

"We'll still call a tow truck, but I don't think the delivery truck coming down the street will be too thrilled that you are blocking his route for however long it takes the tow truck to get here."

I relented and put Velma into neutral. I steered her gently to the side of the road as Anthony and the delivery guy pushed her from behind.

"Thanks," Anthony said as he shook the delivery driver's hand.

"No problem. Happy to help." The driver hopped back in his truck and chugged by me with a wave of his hand.

"Tow truck will be here in fifteen minutes," I said as I disconnected the call and tossed my cell phone back in my purse. "You saved my bacon."

"I love bacon," Anthony said.

"You need to try Nellie Jo's Maple Bacon muffins. They're to die for!" I realized what I said and quickly sobered.

"What's going on, Phee? Surely the Maple Bacon muffins aren't lethal."

"It's not that. Nellie's husband, Mike, was found murdered at the pickle factory. If I don't figure out who killed him soon, the sheriff is going to pin the murder on Nellie. She won't be making Maple Bacon muffins in the big house." I proceeded to bring my day to a grand finale and burst into tears.

Anthony pulled me to him and stroked my hair. "Phee, what's going on? I know you care about Nellie, but it's no reason to cry. She's not in jail, is she?"

"It's not just Nellie. Clint's being an ass and says he doesn't want our relationship to change or move forward. Some hoity-toity federal agent has the hots for him and made me have a unibrow and now Velma is kaput! I need one good thing to happen today!"

"Me."

"What?" I sniffed and gave Anthony a confused look.

"I'm your one good thing that happened today. I'm going to take you to the Senator's cabin and fix you an amazing dinner. We'll listen to music and sing loudly and badly at the top of our lungs. It will be great."

"I don't know," I hesitated. Anthony was a blast and we did have fun when we spent time together, but dinner alone at the cabin was a step I wasn't sure I wanted to take.

"Invite your sister and Wade. It will be fun. I promise," Anthony cajoled.

I hesitated a moment longer. I pushed a lock of hair out of my eye and my fingers brushed the spot where my eyebrow once lived. "Why not? It will be fun. Give me a ride home or are you the kind of guy to leave a girl stranded?"

"My dear. Your chariot awaits."

# CHAPTER ELEVEN

Anthony opened a bottle of Bordeaux and we carried our glasses to the deck to enjoy the view of the lake as the sun began to set.

"So tell me about Nellie and Mike," Anthony said. He sat down next to me on the wooden Adirondack chairs and sipped his wine.

"It turns out Mike wasn't the man that everyone thought he was. Protesters have taken over the town protesting his pickle factory. They're saying he's been dumping pickle brine into the water and causing a fish kill. If that weren't enough, he was cheating on Nellie with a cheap hussy who dances for cash."

Anthony choked on his wine. "Cheap hussy? I don't think I've heard anyone but my grandma use that word."

"Well, she is. Fake boobs and too much makeup. To top it all off, her name is Dusty Rose. What kind of person is named Dusty Rose? What kind of man throws away a wife and family?" I gulped my wine then refilled my glass.

"You're really upset about all of this, aren't you?" Anthony asked. "What's going on with you, Phee?"

I sighed. "Nothing. Everything."

"Is it Clint?"

"Partly. He wants a girlfriend, not a wife and family. I want the house, two kids and the picket fence."

"A lot of guys are skittish when it comes to marriage and children. He could change his mind," Anthony said.

"I don't know that he will, and I don't know that I'm willing to wait until he does," I said. I looked away to hide the tears that threatened to fall. "I want the seven-course meal, not just the appetizer and dessert."

"I get it. Trust me. I really do," Anthony said. He leaned towards me, and for a moment, I thought he was going to kiss me. His eyes met mine and after a moment, he sat back in his chair and propped his feet on the railing. "I don't want to settle for half a seven-course meal either."

A car horn sounded from the front of the house. I heard tires crunch on the driveway. Juliet and Wade had arrived. Relieved to escape what was quickly becoming an uncomfortable moment, I jumped up. "I'll let them in if you want to start the grill."

"Sure," Anthony said, a wry smile flitted across his face.

Juliet came with a bottle of wine in one hand and a chocolate cake in the other. "These count as either inspiration or consolation depending on how your day went," she said.

"Definitely consolation after the day I've had."

Juliet cocked her head and looked at me. "What's up with the bangs? They're cute."

"There was a little mishap at the beauty salon and if I talk about it, I'll cry. My beauty drama trauma will be a sisters only talk. It has been a truly craptastic day."

"I'm sure the mechanic will be able to fix Velma," Wade reassured me.

"Who's going to fix Nellie?" I grabbed the cake from Juliet and led them down the hallway to the deck.

"How's it going?" Wade clapped Anthony on his shoulder. "The Senator keeping you hopping?"

"You know it. Campaign finance reform is the hot topic right now. I eat, sleep and dream election." Anthony pulled up chairs for Wade and Juliet.

"That's not what I want to dream about," Juliet joked. She

leaned down and kissed Wade on his cheek.

"Back at ya, babe." Wade smiled. "Juliet and I compared notes on the way here about Mike's murder. The only thing I heard all day at the library was innuendos that Mike was tied to some shady deals with some of his relatives in Louisiana. Don't know how much is true or if it's just tongues wagging."

"Nellie came to see me today," I said. "She said there is no way Mike could have been killing the fish in the area. He loved to fish and spent a lot of his free time out on the lake. Could the protesters be wrong? Could something else have been causing the fish kill?"

Anthony turned from the grill and said, "I could do a little poking around and help with that. I've got contacts with the EPA and with some of the state inspectors. If Mike's factory was in violation of anything, they would know."

"According to Darcy and Dragonfly, they called the EPA and the agency is backlogged, so no one's been out to investigate," I said.

Anthony arched his eyebrow. "Darcy and Dragonfly?"

"Two of the people protesting Mike's factory," I explained. "I'm bothered by something Oscar said, too. According to him, Mike was a cheat in business. If it's true, then cutting corners and illegally dumping pickle brine makes sense. Plus, Mike seemed to have more money than a pickle business would provide."

"It's almost as if Mike were two different people," Juliet said. "Mr. Beige Husband who liked to fish and didn't bother or make an impact on anyone or anything, and Mr. Creepy Eyes who killed fish, gave me the heebie jeebies and had a stripper girlfriend on the side."

"Despite what you see on television, it's hard to lead two separate lives. Eventually, something unravels or you say the wrong thing at the wrong time and it all crumbles. Nellie must have suspected something," Anthony said. "Dinner's about ready, folks. Who wants cheese on their burger?"

As the burgers were served and the wine was poured, our conversation drifted to other things. Anthony asked Juliet if she still planned on becoming a police officer.

"I don't know," Juliet said. "I actually think I'm better suited to doing something related to the victims of crime or children."

"I have something you might be interested in then," Anthony said. "The Senator and I went to a women's shelter in Burlington a few weeks ago. A number of the women and children were staying there because they were the victims of domestic abuse. Believe it or not, if the judge lets the guy off with a slap on the wrist and a warning not to do it again, the women have no place to go. They end up at a shelter since they don't have the money or the family support to move someplace new."

"That's awful!" Juliet said. "What could I do to help? I'm a yoga instructor, not a counselor."

"Part of the problem is the women are in such shock from their experience that they are having a hard time looking for a new place to live. I thought that a person who could locate homes and apartments available to rent and help the women navigate rental agreements, references and all of the ins and outs of starting over again would be helpful. You're smart and you care. Those two qualities will come in handy working with victims of abuse."

"It sounds challenging," Juliet said slowly. "I'll give it some thought."

"If you decide you want to learn more, call my office and I'll take you to the shelter and introduce you."

"I know some of the guys I served with are dealing with something similar. Some of their problems are related to negotiating life outside of the military and a lot of them are suffering from PTSD, so little things like filling out a job application or a rental agreement is overwhelming."

"I thought there were services out there to help vets transition back into civilian life," I said.

"There are, but the number of vets in need of assistance is overwhelming a lot of our available support system," Anthony said. "A lot of our service members went straight from high school into the military and have never negotiated the ins and outs of civilian life."

"That's something I would definitely be interested in helping with," Juliet said.

"It would be nice if the world was like the movies," I said glumly. "The soldier returns home to the girl who waited faithfully for him and they get married and live happily ever after in a house with a porch and a dog."

"If life were like the movies, the girl would always get the guy and he would bring her flowers, write her poetry and it would be boring," Juliet said. "Life's more interesting with challenges, Phee. You just have to decide whether the challenge is worth it."

"I think we're swimming in dangerous jellyfish territory and I , for one, want cake and wine," Wade interrupted before the mood turned dark. "Anyone else?"

"When life gets tough, the tough get chocolate," I said.

"And wine. Don't forget the wine," Juliet joked. "I would love a slice of cake and a refill, Jeeves." She held her empty wine glass out to him.

"Anything for m'lady," Wade said with a bow of his head.

The mood lightened after that and we spent the next hour

chatting about Juliet's yoga class mishaps and my woes of overdue books and not enough funding. As we stood up to leave, Anthony promised to check into complaints against the pickle factory the following morning.

"If I find out anything, I'll call you," Anthony said, "or I could stop by the library, and we could have lunch together."

"Okay," I said.

"Jellyfish territory," Wade commented under his breath.

"Sometimes you just dive in and hope you don't get stung," I answered.

# CHAPTER TWELVE

Juliet and Wade dropped me off in front of my house. Fritz and Ferdie were waiting at the door for me. I clipped a leash on Fritz to take him for a quick walk around the block. He sniffed and stopped at every bush and tree, so the fifteen minute walk drifted into close to thirty by the time we made it back to the house. As we rounded the corner, I saw Clint's truck idling in my driveway. My breath caught in my chest. I didn't know if I was up to this after the day I'd had.

I hesitated before walking to the truck. Clint shut off the engine and climbed out. He reached out and wrapped his arms around me. I breathed in his scent and some of the awkwardness that had mingled between us floated away on the night breeze.

"It's been a rough couple of days, and I needed to see you," Clint said. He tilted my chin up and kissed me.

"Yes, it has," I agreed. I felt a tingle in my toes as his eyes swept over me.

"Can we go inside?"

I nodded and we walked inside. The little dog darted behind me and whined as he looked at Clint. "It's alright, Fritz. He won't bite."

Clint dropped into a squat and held his hand out palm down. Fritz gave a tentative sniff and licked his hand before wagging his tail. "Where did this little fella come from?"

"He was in my backyard. The vet says he's about six months old."

"I can't believe you have a dog," Clint said. "I thought you were a die-hard cat fan."

"Ferdie's the one who rescued him. He meowed at the back door until I went out and rescued him. It was meant to be," I said as I walked down the hallway to the kitchen. I grabbed a beer out of the refrigerator and handed it to Clint. "You didn't come by to talk about my new dog, though. What's going on with the case?"

Clint grimaced and twisted  the cap off the beer. "I was hoping you'd forget about the case."

"We both know that's about as likely as me giving up mystery novels. So what did Dusty Rose say about Mike?" I poured myself a glass of wine and sat down at the kitchen table.

"She's an interesting character. Not as dumb as she first appears either. She claims that she met Mike at the Lamplighter and he pursued her hot and heavy. She finally gave in when he offered to pay for her boob job." Clint took a swallow of his beer. "Weird thing? Dusty's originally from Louisiana. Not too far from the town Nellie and Mike lived in before they moved here."

"That can't be a coincidence," I said. What were the odds that Dusty didn't know Mike?

"I don't think she's lying about knowing Mike from before. Think about it. Mike's in his late fifties. Dusty is in her twenties. She would have been a child when Nellie and Mike lived there."

"True. It's still an odd coincidence."

"Dusty Rose isn't her real name either." Clint took his hat off and placed it on the table. He ran his hand through his hair. "Her real name is Regina Diller."

"No wonder she changed it. Dusty Rose is definitely a better stage name. If I was going to be a pole dance, I'd call myself Foxy Vixen or Smoky Foxx."

"You aren't planning a career change anytime soon are you? If you are, you might want to rethink those names," Clint chuckled.

"No immediate career changes planned so I'll stick with Phee for the time being. So what did Dusty aka Regina say she was doing at the factory the night Mike died?" I asked.

"She claims she went there to break things off with him, but Mike had another woman in his office. Dusty went off in a tizzy that Mike would have another woman at their special place. Those were her words, not mine."

"I call bull pucky on her story that she went there to break things off with him. She works in a fleabag dive bar where the tips can't be that good. Mike was the gravy on her gnarly mashed potato life. She told Juliet and me that she loved Mike."

"About you and Juliet's visit to the Lamplighter…" Clint started.

"I know what you're going to say. You're going to say that we need to leave the investigation to the professionals and stick to books and yoga mats," I said in my best imitation of Clint's voice.

"Yes, you should leave it to the professionals, but what I was going to say is that's not the place a nice girl like you should go. There are some dangerous characters that drink there – biker gangs on their way to the bike rallies in Burlington, petty drug dealers and other guys you never want to take home to your mother. Please don't go there again. For me." He gave me a pleading look.

If he could have pulled off sad puppy eyes, I think he would have. As it was, I had no immediate plans to return to the illustrious Lamplighter Lounge. "No problem. I'll stay away. What I'm wondering is why Mike would have gone into such a rat's nest. It's not like he didn't have the funds to go to a better location. Heck. If he wanted to drink, it's not like he couldn't go to Burlington or even to Carbuncle's Cabana on the Cove."

"From my talk with the bartender, Mike sometimes met people there. It sounds like he used the place to conduct business meetings. Guess the pickle business is a little rough around the edges."

I gave a bark of laughter at the thought of Mike and a group of men in suits and ties talking pickles while a stripper danced trying to get a rise out of their other pickle. "I'm having a hard time reconciling soft-spoken Mike, husband, fisherman and grandpa, with a beer-swilling letch who went to Lamplighter's and had a mistress named Dusty Rose."

"People never know what goes on behind closed doors. People always think folks are Ozzie and Harriet, when in reality they're Dan and Roseanne," Clint said wryly. "I should know because I'm the one who sees the dark side of families and couples." A flash of pain crossed his face before he looked away.

I reached out and grabbed his hand. "I've missed you."

Clint said and pulled me over onto his lap. He kissed me lightly on my nose then his lips moved to mine. He said huskily, "I've missed you, too."

"There's a way to remedy that," I said softly thinking we could continue this conversation in my bedroom.

Clint stopped kissing my neck. "We've been down this road and I'm not changing my mind. I don't want to live with anyone or marry anyone, period." His voice was tight and tinged with anger.

I stood up startled that he misunderstood my intention. I walked to the sink to hide the tears welling in my eyes. "I think you should leave."

"Phee…"

"Please leave," I whispered, tears flowing freely down my cheeks. "I love you, Clint, but I need you to leave and give me time to think. I want the Ozzie and Harriet dream. You don't. Message received. Please go."

Clint put a hand on my shoulder and tried to pull me to him, but I resisted. He dropped his hand. A minute later, I heard the front door close.

Fritz sat at my feet and whined. I stroked his fuzzy head. "It looks like it's just you, me and the cat, boy."

# CHAPTER THIRTEEN

Staring in the mirror the next morning, my puffy eyes and red nose attested to my sleepless night. I stood in the hot shower a long time letting the steam and water wash away the harsh reality of Clint's words and my decision to walk away from the love of my life.

I thought of Margaret Mitchell's *Gone with the Wind*, "I made a pretty suit of clothes and fell in love with it. And when Ashley came riding along, so handsome, so different, I put that suit on him and made him wear it whether it fitted him or not. And I wouldn't see what he really was. I kept on loving the pretty clothes—and not him at all," I quoted as I patted concealer to hide my dark circles.

I pulled a black turtleneck over my head and slipped on a pair of black slacks. My outfit matched my dark mood. I dug around in my purse for my keys before I remembered Velma was at the shop getting fixed. I headed out the door to walk to work.

I made it to Main Street in ten minutes. I glanced down the block and saw lights on and cars in front of Nellie Jo's Cup o' Joe. Detouring away from the library, I headed to the coffee shop. Aside from wanting to check on Nellie, I desperately needed a strong cup of coffee and a chocolate chip muffin.

I pushed the door open expecting to hear the familiar hum of voices and the rich smell of coffee and baked goods. Instead, there was a palpable tension and eyes turned awkwardly away from the scene unfolding at the cash register.

"I don't care what you think you had with my husband, but

I can guarantee you were nothing but a two-bit piece of cheap carpet he wanted to lay and then wipe his feet on!" Nellie spat out the words. She glared across the counter at Dusty.

"Well, let me tell you something, lady, this cheap carpet excited him more than the old cracked linoleum he had at home. I'm an upgrade!" Dusty snapped back and chomped her gum angrily.

Eddie tugged at Dusty's arm. "Listen, Dusty, now isn't the time or the place for this. Uncle Mike wouldn't want this."

"I think I know what Mike would have wanted more than you." Dusty yanked her arm from Eddie's grip and stalked out of the shop. She yanked the door so hard the bell gave a discordant jangle of protest.

"Aunt Nellie, I'll handle this. Don't even worry about her," Eddie said to Nellie before jogging after Dusty.

I watched through the window as Eddie and Dusty exchanged words. Whatever Eddie said to her must have calmed her down because before they walked off down the sidewalk, I saw Dusty reach out and touch Eddie's hand in a conciliatory gesture. Interesting.

"I'm sorry you folks had to see that," Nellie said to the customers who were busy looking everywhere but at Nellie. "Guess I shoulda stayed closed for a few more days to let the dust settle and sort out Mike's affairs." She grimaced when she realized what she'd said.

"Nellie, can I get two coffees to go with a shot of chocolate in one and two chocolate chip muffins, please," I said loudly to break the awkward silence.

"Sure thing," Nellie said. "Wade likes a little touch of chocolate in his coffee, too. Want me to add a shot to both?"

"Sure," I said. I leaned over the counter and whispered, "How are you holding up?"

"I'm doing alright," Nellie said quietly. "I'd be doing better if folks would stop acting like I got the pox."

"Nellie, I need to know more about Mike's business dealings. I've done a little digging around and some people say that not all the money came from the pickle business. Is there something you're not telling me about Mike?"

Nellie picked up a rag and wiped the counter in front of me. Without meeting my eyes, she said, "I tried to not ask too many questions when it came to Mike's business dealings. I like my little coffee shop and muffin baking. Pickles are great for eating, but I don't need to know the ins and outs of making them. We brought a little nest egg with us when we moved here. It gave us a start."

Clearly, Nellie was dancing around how Mike made his money. I decided to try another route. "What did you and Mike do before you moved to Miller's Cove? You lived in Louisiana before this, didn't you?"

"Sure did. Mike worked for his family's business before we decided to move here. We thought it would be a better environment for our boy. Better schools. Cleaner air."

"What was the family business?"

Nellie stopped wiping the counter. She turned away from me and poured coffee into two cups. "You said two cups of coffee and two muffins, right?"

Nellie was hiding something as sure as the chocolate chips in her muffins were hiding their calorie count. I didn't think I could learn anything more at this point. "That's right. Two shots of chocolate, too, please."

"Coming right up," When she placed my order in front of me, her hands were shaking slightly. Lowering her voice, she said, "Phee, forget about looking into Mike's murder. I'm sure the police will figure out that I had nothing to do with it.

Problem solved. I appreciate everything you've done, but it was silly of me to ask you to do this."

"You're my friend, Nellie," I said and reached out and placed my hand over hers. "Don't worry about me. I'll be fine. I'm just asking a few questions and checking out alibis."

"I asked you to stop and if you're my friend you'll do as I ask and stop poking your nose into my business," Nellie said harshly. "No charge for the coffee and muffins. You'd better get on to work and shelve some books." She turned around and began to fiddle with the coffee machine.

Bewildered by her sudden change of heart, I waited a moment to see if she would say anything else. When she continued humming to herself and wiping at nonexistent dirt on the coffee machines, I sighed and picked up my order to go. "I'll see you later, Nellie. Call me if you need anything."

"Bye," Nellie responded without her usual warmth.

Something was wrong with my friend. Despite her dismissal of my help, I was going to find out what was behind her reticence to talk about Mike's business dealings. When the going gets tough, the tough go to the library to dig up clues!

# CHAPTER FOURTEEN

Once I'd finished my daily opening routine at the library, I settled down at my computer to use some of the online resources and databases. If there was anything in public files on Mike and his pickle business, this librarian was going to find it.

I started off simple with the Secretary of State's website. I found the corporate filings for the pickle factory. I noted that the state of incorporation was Louisiana. That made sense since Mike and Nellie moved to Miller's Cove from there. I surfed around some of the government and business resources I liked to use to see if Mike had any complaints against him. After fifteen minutes of searching, I hadn't found any complaints filed against the pickle factory for illegal dumping and the pickles were popular with restaurants in the state. All the reviews of Mike's pickle products were glowing. Seems like he might have actually made his money with pickles.

I decided to dig a little deeper. I searched the newspaper database which archived newspapers from around the country. It even carried some from other countries. Bingo! There were numerous results from newspapers in Louisiana and eastern Texas. Opening up the first hit, I couldn't believe what I read. I decided to print the articles to show to Juliet. As the printer hummed to life, the door to the library opened and the first patron of the day walked in. The investigation would have to wait.

I spent the morning working on a genealogy request from an out-of-state patron who had called. Her great-grandfather had settled in Miller's Cove back in the 1920s. She wanted me to find an obituary, and if possible, any information related to other relatives in the area. By the time Wade came in at noon, my head was spinning from searching through reels of microfilm for any information on Jebediah Orr.

"What's up?" Wade greeted me.

"I would love it if the local newspaper would digitize their collection so I wouldn't have to suffer vertigo looking for obituaries," I complained. "On the flip side, microfilm and ancestor hunting keep small libraries like this in business, so I shouldn't complain." I stretched my arms over my head and groaned. My neck and shoulders protested after sitting hunched over the machine so long.

"Did you find what you were looking for?" Wade asked as he checked in the books that were in the book drop.

"Somewhat. I found the obituary the patron wanted and some interesting information about his life. Turns out Mr. Orr was married not once, but twice."

"That's not unusual. Widowers usually remarried quickly. It's not like men during that era took care of their children on their own. There was usually a nice spinster lady who would eagerly step in to the role of Mrs. Orr."

"That's not what's interesting," I said. "It turns out that the first Mrs. Orr didn't die. She was institutionalized soon after giving birth to Jebediah Orr, Jr. She probably had post-partum depression."

"Maybe," Wade agreed, "but times were different. For all we know, she could have gone crazy and tried to hurt the baby."

"The most interesting thing I found out was that Jebediah Senior conveniently forgot to divorce the first Mrs. Orr before marrying wife number two. I guess it was a case of out of sight, out of mind. Wife number one was eventually released from the sanitarium and came home to find wife number two raising her child. Needless to say, things got ugly."

"I bet they did. Are you sending all of the newspaper articles to the patron about the wives, or are you going to play it safe and just send the obituary?" Wade asked. He knew that genealogists didn't always like what they found out about their long-lost relatives.

"I'm sending it all. She might like to know. She asked me to find out more information and I did." I placed the printouts from the microfilm in a large envelope and sealed it. The mail had already come today, so I'd mail it in the morning. "I found out some interesting information about Mike."

"What?" Wade stopped sorting the books on the cart and gave me his full attention.

"Oh no. Juliet would kill me if I let the cat out of the bag without her. Let's all go to Odd Couple's after work. I'll show you what I found then."

"Tease!" Wade joked. "Five o'clock can't come soon enough."

Wade and I were busy the rest of the afternoon. I had my afterschool story hour and the phone rang throughout the day with reference requests. By the time the last patron exited the library, we were exhausted.

"I don't think we've been this busy in a while," Wade said as he turned the lights off in the reading area.

"I guess you're too tired to go out to eat," I teased.

"Nice try. I survived on MRE's and three hours of sleep for nine months. Let's go and meet Juliet. Whatever you found better be good."

"Oh, it is," I said as I locked the front door behind me and headed down the steps.

Fifteen minutes later, Juliet strolled into the diner. "What's up, my people," she greeted us. "I've got news."

"Me, too," I responded.

Juliet shrugged off her light jacket and slid into the booth next to Wade. She gave him a light peck on the cheek. "I drove by the pickle factory today. The protesters are still marching in front and calling for a shutdown of pickle production. I thought with Mike dead, the factory would shut down, but his nephew Eddie appears to be running the show now."

"I'm actually glad they didn't shut down," Wade said. "I know a couple of guys who work there. They need their jobs to feed their families. If the factory shuts down, they don't have a lot of options for factory jobs around Miller's Cove."

"That's not the most interesting thing though," Juliet continued. "I saw Dusty Rose at the factory. She was standing outside talking to Eddie. From the view I had, they are good friends."

"Holy guacamole on a chip! So you think Eddie knew his uncle was cheating? I get the willies just thinking about that family dynamic!" I shivered at the thought.

"I could be wrong," Juliet said. "She could be a friendly girl all the time, not just when she's dancing on a pole."

I pretended to gag. "I found out some things, too. It sheds some light on Mike and his money."

I pulled the sheaf of papers I'd printed earlier out of my bag and placed them on the table. I sorted through them to find the earliest newspaper article.

"Hey there. Mind if we join you?"

I glanced up from my documents to see Anthony and Lu standing by our table. "Perfect," I said. "I've got something I want to show you." I slid over to make room for them.

"You haven't been poking around in Mike's murder have

you?" Lu gave me an interrogating glare.

"Kind of, sort of, maybe," I said guiltily. "In my defense, I did research at the library. That doesn't count as investigating. It was reference work."

"Hmmm…I guess I'll let that slide. Clint's worried you might stick your nose into a hornet's nest of trouble. Our victim wasn't the boring pickle purveyor we thought he was," Lu said. She opened her menu.

"I'll wait until we've ordered before sharing," I said.

Wade groaned. "The suspense is killing me. Juls, you're sister's been the proverbial cat who swallowed the canary all day."

"She's like that," Juliet agreed. "You should have grown up with her. She would sneak around and find all of our Christmas presents hidden in the house and then drop hints without telling Rick and me."

"Serves you right for not helping to find them," I shot back. "Anthony, where did you run into Lu? At the station? Is something up with the Senator?"

"No, nothing like that. I'm on vacation this week, remember. Lu and I've kept in touch since my last visit here. We've chatted online a bit. Turns out she owns the one and only CD my band released. I have some tickets to see a rockabilly group that's playing at the state fairgrounds this weekend, and I went by the station to see if she wanted to go."

"I adore Hot Fish on a Griddle," Lu said.

"Is that the name of the band or what you want to eat for dinner?" Juliet asked. She wiggled her eyebrows at me and did a slight nod towards Anthony and Lu. I gave her an "I don't know" shrug.

"The band," Lu said. "They're from Long Island. I used to see them when I was back home."

The waitress came and took our orders. Once she left, I held up my first discovery from earlier in the day. "You guys aren't going to believe what I found. Mike Johnson was in the mafia!"

# CHAPTER FIFTEEN

Anthony let out a long, low whistle. "Whoa. That's a big accusation, Phee. What do you have to back it up?"

"Mafia? Flea, you've clearly been reading too many true crime novels lately. Either that or watched The Godfather recently. If Mike Johnson was a wise guy, I'll wash Velma every week for a year," Juliet said.

Lu didn't say a word. Her lips tightened and she looked out the window, avoiding my eyes.

"Lu? I'm right and you know it," I said.

"I can't comment on an ongoing case. If you were smart, you and your sister will leave this case alone. It's not time for junior crime busters. The mafia is not anything to joke about or poke your noses around if you aren't a trained professional."

"Wait. You mean Mike was in the mafia?" Anthony asked.

Lu stayed silent. After a moment, I decided enough was enough. If there was organized criminal activity in Miller's Cove, the townspeople needed to know. "Mike Johnson was part of the Cajun mafia. They originated out of Louisiana, but they expanded into parts of Texas."

"Holy crap on a cracker! You're serious, aren't you?" Juliet gave me a wide-eyed stare. "What do they do? Feed their hits to the alligators?"

"It's not a joke!" Lu burst out. "That's exactly what they do. You cross these guys and you end up in a swamp as gator bait. It's what makes it so hard to prosecute them. No witnesses because they've been killed. No bodies because they've been eaten."

"We don't have gators around here," I replied. "From what I learned, Mike used to be a heavy hitter with them down in Louisiana. He was busted thirty years ago for money laundering and did five years in the federal penitentiary. When he got out, he and Nellie moved here and as far as I can tell, he's been keeping his nose clean. Maybe he hid all the money he embezzled and that's how they bought the factory."

"Nose clean?" Juliet snickered. "And you mock me for my seventies cop show lingo?"

"You know what I mean. I found all of these newspaper articles from the eighties when he was busted. The rest of his family still live in Louisiana and are still heavily involved in the mafia."

"Which is why you need to leave it alone and let Clint and I handle this. We have the FBI working with us and the last thing we need is amateur hour fouling the investigation," Lu said.

She looked like she wanted to say something more, but our food arrived and she stayed silent. When the waitress left, Lu leaned forward and said in a low voice, "You guys really need to listen to me. Mike Johnson and his family are not a joke. They are bad people and they do bad things. Mike may cleaned up his act once he moved to Miller's Cove, but you can never truly get rid of your past. It looks like Mike's past came back to bite him in his proverbial butt."

"Phee, you should listen to Lu. She knows what she's talking about," Anthony said.

I held up my hands in defeat. "I'm not going to interfere in the investigation. Nellie asked me to leave it alone, and I am. I'm just sharing what I found out."

Lu eyed me dubiously. "Somehow I have a feeling that you're still going to poke around and get into trouble. It's your shtick."

"I don't have a shtick," I said defensively. "I just like digging up the facts. That's what librarians do."

"Well, stick to facts for school projects. Let the cops dig for the truth on this one," Lu said.

"I will. I promise." I said. I crossed my fingers under the table. I didn't plan on looking for more information, but if I stumbled across any while I was out and about, I wanted to cover my bases.

By unspoken agreement, we changed the subject and talked about other things. Anthony told a funny story about when he toured with his rockabilly band, and Lu shared some of her escapades when she was a rookie cop. The tension from earlier eased as our plates eventually emptied.

Wade pushed his plate away and patted his flat stomach. "I'm so stuffed I feel like a Thanksgiving turkey."

"You're a turkey alright," Juliet joked. "I can't eat another bite. I want to go home and be a sloth on the couch."

"I had the same idea. I'm going to get into my pj's and read a book. I  ate enough for a week," I groaned.

"Well, I wish I could say that I could, but unfortunately, we have some meeting with the FBI agent here. She's supposed to be some kind of expert on money laundering and financial crimes."

"Her name wouldn't be Elizabeth Shields, would it?" I asked.

"Sure is. How did you know? Have you met her?" Lu asked.

"In a manner of speaking," I replied. I could feel my blood pressure rising as I recalled our "meeting" at the beauty shop the other day. I reached up and flipped my long swooped bangs out of my face to reveal my missing eyebrow. "Elizabeth Shields assaulted my eyebrow and left me with a unibrow!"

"Holy hairy moly!" Juliet exclaimed. "I wondered what was up with the hair and the weird eyebrow thing, but I thought you had a plucking accident or something. What on earth happened?"

I told them of my run in at Tinted Love with Agent Shields. "Now I look like some kind of freak with only one eyebrow. That woman might be an expert on financial shenanigans, but that has nothing to do with me. I have no idea why she "accidentally on purpose" marred me."

"I think I may know why," Lu said. "Elizabeth Shields is newly divorced and on the prowl. She has Clint in her crosshairs and you're standing in her way."

"Me? I doubt it. Clint's told me in no uncertain terms that he doesn't want to settle down, so as far as I'm concerned, he is welcome to date her if he wants." Even as I said the words, a knife turned in my gut and my dinner became a leaden mass.

"She's a witch with a capital 'B'," Lu said. "If that's what Clint wants in a woman, then I'll eat my badge."

"I appreciate your loyalty. I have no idea what Clint wants at this point," I said. I threw my napkin on my plate and stood up. "I'm tired and stuffed to the gills. I'll see you tomorrow. The walk home will do me some good."

I left the restaurant and walked down the street towards home. As the sun set and the houses and shops around Miller's Cove lit up for the evening, I glanced around my hometown. What other secrets did the friends and families I knew and loved have? Would I ever look at this place the same?

# CHAPTER SIXTEEN

I wanted to sleep in the next morning, but my cell phone ringing at five o'clock decided it was time for me to wake up.

"Hello?" I sat up in my bed. I rubbed the sleep from my eyes. Ferdinand protested my pushing him off my feet with a grouchy meow.

"Wakey wakey! It's yoga time!" Juliet's perky voice penetrated the cobwebs of sleep that lingered.

"Really? How are you my sister? Do you realize what time it is?" I grumbled.

"As a matter of fact, I do. It's time for Phee to get up and get dressed because her beautiful, vivacious and talented sister will be there in thirty minutes to ensure that you stay healthy and maintain balance in your life," Juliet said. Her cheerfulness this early in the morning made me want to throw a book at her. A heavy book. A heavy book with big words.

"Alright. Since I'm awake, I might as well go with you," I sighed. "See you in half an hour."

I stumbled out of bed. I started my coffee pot to perking while I let Fritz out for his morning jaunt around the yard. He chased a few bugs and sniffed every tree and bush before bouncing back inside to eat his chow.

"I think you and Juliet share the same batteries," I said to Fritz. "You keep going and going while the rest of us are ready to power down."

I poured my cup of coffee and went to grab my morning paper. The paper boy had once again missed my porch. I walked barefoot around to my rosebushes and gingerly reached my hand and grabbed the paper from the thorny branches. When I straightened up, a slip of paper fluttered from the folds of the newspaper. Had I forgotten to pay this month's subscription and needed a reminder note? I opened the folded paper. *Keep your nose out of other folk's business.*

I stood shocked for a minute as I wrapped my head around the idea that someone had sent me a nasty note. How did they know that the paper would be mine? Did Jimmy the newspaper boy put the note in there or had someone snuck down my sidewalk to tuck it in there? Was the note meant for me or perhaps someone was tired of Oscar and his nosiness? I felt dizzy from all the possibilities.

I scurried back inside and slammed the door shut behind me. A moment ago, I had been frightened as the note brought back the memory of the night a killer had left a warning for me at my home. Now, I was angry. Someone had snuck a note like a coward to warn me away from helping my friend. Well, they could kiss my slightly-large rear end!

I grabbed my cup of coffee and settled down at the kitchen table to drink it while glancing at the headlines from the morning's paper. According to the sheriff, there were no new leads in Mike's murder, but they were "pursuing several lines of enquiries." I knew from my conversations with Clint that it was a standard line to allay the public's fears when the sheriff had reached dead ends and was stuck on where to go in an investigation.

I glanced up at the clock on my wall. Juliet would be here in less than fifteen minutes. I hurried into my yoga clothes and was tying my hair up into a high ponytail when I heard Juliet knocking on the door. I grabbed my yoga mat and giving Fritz a quick pat on the head and a promise to return shortly, I ran out to meet her.

"Good morning, Merry Sunshine!" Juliet chirped as she jumped into the driver's seat of her convertible.

"You do realize how annoying you are to ninety-nine percent of the population who are not early morning people, don't you?"

"Yes, but I'm working on converting at least half of them to my way of thinking so I don't care." She pulled out of my driveway and headed towards the community center at the lake.

"Someone left me a nasty note with my morning paper," I said nonchalantly.

"What?" Juliet swerved as she took her eyes off the road to look at me. "Oh my goddess! Why are you so calm? What did it say?"

"It told me to quit nosing around other people's business," I said. "Not really a threat. More like a coward trying to frighten me away from the investigation."

"Well, they don't have to worry about it anyway since our conversation with Lu yesterday. Besides, Nellie doesn't want you looking into it anymore. Problem solved."

"Maybe," I said slowly. "Think about it. I'm just a librarian, but clearly something I've uncovered or learned has someone nervous. I doubt the sheriff or Clint are receiving threats. Why me?"

"Most criminals are smart enough not to send threats to the law, Phee."

"True. For all I know they meant it to go to Oscar. Now that I realize how much he knows about everyone in town and all their dirty little secrets, I'm tempted to send him a note myself to mind his own bee's wax." I imagined Oscar's face if he received an anonymous note. "I shouldn't be so mean. I suppose if I was mayor and needed to be successful as a politician and business owner, I might be nosy, too."

"Maybe," Juliet said slowly. "I think you should lay low. See if Lu and Clint find out any more information about Mike and his ties to the Cajun mafia."

"I'm only going to do some librarian sleuthing. Strictly looking up newspaper articles. Plus, I had no idea about fish kills. I'm curious to learn more about Darcy and her protesting posse."

"I can help you out with that one," Juliet said as she pulled her convertible up in front of the community center and killed the engine. "I invited the protesters to yoga class, and it looks like at least some of them took me up on my offer of a free introductory session."

I looked to where Juliet indicated and spotted Darcy, Dragonfly and Willow huddled together by the door. Grabbing my mat, I ambled over to them. "Good morning," I greeted them. "I see Juliet twisted your arms to make you come to what I call her butt crack o' dawn class."

"We're early risers anyway," Dragonfly said solemnly. Did the woman ever smile? She seemed so serious, but I guess saving the environment was fairly serious business.

"The early protester gets the best spot," Darcy said. "After years of doing this, I've discovered that if you show up once the workers have already arrived for their shift, then your message loses some of its impact. We hit early and often."

"Have you had any success with protests?" I asked.

"Oh, sure. We shut down a factory that was burying barrels of sludge that contained mercury and other nasty crud. We also stopped a coal mine that did mountain top removal. The runoff from their operations spoiled the water for a dozen small towns below them," Darcy said.

"Let's get inside," I said. "My sister might be all sweet with karmic goodness, but she's a stickler for starting class on time."

Darcy and Dragonfly opened the door and went inside. Willow grabbed my arm. "The spirit guides told me to speak to you," Willow said quietly. "Meet me at the picnic table after class. I told the others I had some stones of wisdom for you to add to your pouch so they won't be suspicious."

"Okay," I said. What in the world did Willow have to tell me that she didn't want Darcy and Dragonfly to know? I followed her inside and rolled my mat out at the back of the class.

Over the next few minutes, more early birds wandered in and Juliet started the class. As I moved my body through the sun salutations and various introductory poses, I felt my energy increasing and my tension from the night before melting away. Maybe Juliet was on to something with her exercise and meditative woo woo. By the time the class was over, I felt looser and ready to start the day with a positive attitude. I wiped my mat with one of the cloths provided and rolled it up.

"Hey, Phee," Willow called. "I need to grab those stones for you from my car. Can you wait a few minutes for me?"

"Sure," I said in my "this wasn't planned" voice. "Thanks for remembering them. I'll meet you outside in a minute."

"Great! Darcy, you guys can go ahead without me. I'll meet you at the factory," Willow said. She waved goodbye to her friends and made her way outside.

I took a minute to gather my things together and walked out to the picnic table where Willow waited for me.

"What's up?" I said.

"I overheard something and I wasn't sure what to do with the information," Willow said quietly.

"Is it something that Clint and Lu should know? If so, you should tell them," I said.

"I don't want to be a rat to my friends, so I consulted the spirits. They said I should tell you and you would know what to do."

Willow and her total reliance on her spirit guides could be annoying at times, but she or they had been right on a couple of occasions. "Okay. What is it?"

"I overheard Darcy and Dragonfly talking. They thought I was sleeping. I invited them to stay at my place when I found out they were camping out in a tent with no water or anything. Back to nature is great, but even I appreciate a daily shower and a hot meal.

"Anyway, I heard Darcy saying that it was an accident and she hadn't meant to shove him. She said Mike was rubbing his head and cursing at her when she left."

"Holy guacamole, Willow! You shouldn't keep this to yourself. The sheriff needs to know this stuff. Maybe Mike was injured and fell into the pickle vat. If that's the case, it wasn't murder."

"I know, but what if I heard wrong? Plus, the spirits told me you would know what to do with the information. I don't want Darcy to go to jail. It might not be murder, but they could still charge her with a crime."

I realized Willow was right. The district attorney would probably want to at least charge her with assault or possibly even manslaughter. "I have to think about this. I don't feel comfortable not telling Clint or Lu. Let me see if I can find out more information before I bring in the police. Did you ask Darcy about it?"

"I almost did, but I just…" Willow trailed off. "I believe in what they're doing, Phee. Mike and his pickle factory have dumped thousands of gallons of brine into the streams that feed the lake. Who knows how much damage has been done.

I'm not saying he deserved to die, but he needed to be stopped."

Willow was correct when she said Mike needed to be stopped if he was dumping brine into the streams. Darcy shouldn't have taken the law into her own hands though. I knew that I had to share this information with Clint. He might not want to talk to me about our relationship, but he couldn't avoid a concerned citizen sharing information about an ongoing investigation.

I told Willow I would think about what to do and headed to the car. Juliet waited in the driver's seat and once we were on the road back to my house, she asked me why Willow and I were deep in conversation when she came outside. "She wasn't trying to convince you to do a cosmic cleansing again, was she?"

"No, nothing like that. I wish it was that easy," I replied. I was still troubled by what I'd learned. I relayed what Willow had heard. "I'm going to shower and head into town early to talk to Clint before work."

"I'll go with you," Juliet offered. "With Velma on the fritz and rain in the forecast, I will play chauffeur to your Miss Daisy."

"You are the best sister ever," I said.

"I'm your only sister, so it was an easy popularity contest."

When we got to my house, Juliet played with Fritz in the backyard while I showered and got dressed for work. I pulled on a pair of black plants with a cute flare at the bottom and some ballet slipper flats. A polka-dot tie front blouse completed my outfit. I twisted my hair into a bun and pulled my bangs down over my unibrow. I cursed Agent Shields again under my breath. She better hope my eyebrow grows back. Otherwise, she and I would have words.

Juliet drove me to the sheriff's office. She and I went inside, and I let Tina know that I was there to see Clint.

Tina chomped her gum. "He's in a meeting right now with that FBI agent, Elizabeth Shields." The note of contempt in her voice when she said the name made me like Tina a little bit more. Glad to know I wasn't the only one who wasn't a fan.

"I'll wait." I sat down on one of the hard plastic chairs in the lobby and crossed my legs.

"Me, too," Juliet said. "I don't have another class for an hour, so I have time to kill."

The minutes ticked slowly by as I imagined Agent Shields cooing over Clint's every word. Not that I cared. He and I were in limbo status. I had options. I could date other guys. After all, there were plenty of single guys who wanted a committed relationship. Problem was, they weren't in Miller's Cove. The pool of possible love interests was a population of none. Sighing, I looked at Juliet and said, "I can't wait much longer. I'm opening the library this morning. I'm supposed to let Charlie in so he can take the garbage out, too."

"Five more minutes and we'll go. He can come to the library to talk to you. I would like to scope out Agent Shields. I'm curious to see who assaulted your eyebrows."

"Hardy har har. You're such a laugh riot," I said.

Charlie Cochran burst through the doors. "I need to talk to someone right now," Charlie panted. He leaned over to catch his breath and then said, "I think Nellie's been kidnapped!"

# CHAPTER SEVENTEEN

Pandemonium broke out. Tina shouted towards the back of the sheriff's office for someone to come up front.

"What do you mean Nellie's been kidnapped?" I demanded, grasping Charlie by the elbow and guiding him to a nearby chair. With his heart condition, Charlie couldn't handle stress. "Sit down and talk to me."

"I went by to pick Nellie up this morning to bring her to work," Charlie explained. "The sheriff has her car impounded while they look for evidence that she killed Mike." He glared at Clint as he emerged from the back office.

"Tina said Nellie's missing," Clint said. "Charlie, you need to come back in my office and make a report. Phee, I'll handle this. You and Juliet can leave now."

"I'm not going anywhere," I said. I stood between Charlie and Clint. "Nellie's my friend, and I want to know what's going on."

"You need to keep your girlfriend under control, Clint. This is an ongoing FBI investigation and you small-town cops have allowed amateur hour to go on for far too long," Elizabeth said as she emerged from the back office. She looked me up and down. Her lip curled in contempt. Her navy blue suit was impeccably cut to show off her figure.

I bared my teeth in a forced smile and said, "This amateur knows a thing or two about finding out the truth. Miller's Cove is my home. We all live here and work together. When a member of our family is in trouble, we all help. As far as I'm concerned, Nellie's family. If you can't accept that then maybe they need to send another agent."

"Oh, it bites when it's cornered. I hope you had a recent rabies shot," Agent Shields gave me a condescending smile. "Clint, I'll see you and our witness in the back conference room in five minutes." She turned on her heels and strode out of the reception area, her black heels clicking loudly.

Juliet began to hum the witch's tune from the *Wizard of Oz* under her breath. "Dum da dum da dum dum. Dum da dum da dum dum."

Clint gave me a tired look and ran his fingers through his dark hair. "Phee, I need you to leave. End of discussion."

"Can I…" I began, but Clint held up his hand to stop me.

"No. I'm done talking about this. There are things going on here that I can't talk to you about and you don't need to know. All you're doing right now is interfering with an active investigation. If you keep at it, I'll have to arrest you."

"You'll arrest my sister over my dead body!" Juliet spat. "To think that I considered you part of my family. Come on, Phee. Let's go."

Reluctantly, I gave Charlie a pat on his shoulder and told him I would check on him later. I gave Clint one last angry glare and stalked out of the sheriff's office.

"The nerve of that woman!" Juliet practically shouted. "I wanted to take her badge and shove it…"

"I'll be right beside you to help," I said. "There's something going on in our little town, and it's not good." I hitched my purse onto my shoulder and walked down the block towards the library.

"That's all you've got to say? You're going to just leave and go to work?"

"I am." I kept walking at a brisk pace, anger fueling me forward.

"You're going to give up and leave Nellie to the wolves?"

"Certainly not. Where do you think the first place Charlie's will go to once Clint's done taking a report?"

"Ah, wise one. Grasshopper bows to your greater wisdom and all-knowing ways," Juliet nodded her head. "Charlie's going to come straight to the library whether Clint Mason likes it or not. Last I heard, Miller's Cove is still a free country and not under martial law."

"Well, we're actually an incorporated township, but I get what you're trying to say," I said. "Listen, I need you to do me a favor today."

"Sure," Juliet said. "If it helps Nellie, I'm all in. Forget what I said yesterday about playing it safe. No one takes our Nellie and gets away with it."

"I can't leave the library today. I need you to do some gentle digging around with the protesters. Something's not adding up with Darcy and her crew. I want to know what actually happened between Darcy and Mike Sunday night and why she pushed him. Maybe his death really was a horrible accident, or maybe Darcy and her group aren't the peace-loving hippies they claim to be."

"Aye, aye, Cap'n." Juliet saluted me. "Promise you'll call me as soon as you learn anything about Nellie."

"I promise. For now, keep Nellie's disappearance under wraps. Charlie might have gotten confused about what day to pick up Nellie. You know how forgetful he is sometimes."

"I hope so," Juliet said, "but somehow I have a feeling he got it right this time. I'll see you later."

"I'll call as soon as I've talked to Charlie." I unlocked the front door to the library and turned on the lights.

I only had five minutes until opening, so I hustled to get everything ready for the day. I pushed the cart to the overnight drop and gathered the few books out of the bottom. As I wheeled back to the circulation desk, I turned on all of the computers in the lab. I had less than a minute before opening, and I hadn't broken a sweat. A small victory in my library world.

The next hour passed quickly as my regulars came to pick up the books that had been placed on hold for them. A few of them didn't even bother to request items anymore since I knew what they liked to read and did it automatically. Despite the current crime wave, I loved Miller's Cove. If I worked in a big city library, I wouldn't be able to do this level of customer service. I knew Tommy Timberlake was on book eighteen of the Hardy Boys series. He insisted on reading them in order. I already knew what I would recommend after he finished the series. I always put the latest James Patterson and Jeffery Deaver aside for Mrs. Wright. She picked them up on time and returned them early since she knew others were waiting for them. I worried that organized crime had wheedled its way into my hometown and it would never be the same.

At eleven o'clock, Charlie entered the library. His face was flushed. He looked around anxiously until he spotted me at the microfilm machine. I asked my morning volunteer to watch the desk and motioned Charlie into my office.

"Phee, I tell you that man of yours has me fuming," Charlie declared as soon as I shut the door.

"I feel the same way about him sometimes. Tell me what happened."

Charlie sat down in the chair next to my desk. "Something's happened to Nellie. I feel it in my bones. I got to her place at six o'clock to pick her up. She wanted to come into town to check on the coffee shop and make sure the part-time gal she has working there could handle things on her own for the next day or so. The front door was locked, the lights were off, and Nellie was nowhere to be found. I went out to the stables, the garage, everywhere. No Nellie. I guarantee whoever killed Mike has Nellie."

"It does sound suspicious," I agreed. "Maybe she forgot you were coming by to pick her up."

"No way. I talked to her last night right before I went to watch my favorite episode of *Barnaby Jones*. She reminded me to pick her up. Phee, I'm worried." He wrung his Cincinnati Red's baseball cap between his hands.

I patted his shoulder to try to calm him down. "It'll be okay, Charlie. I'm sure Clint will put out a missing person's alert and every police officer in the state will be looking for Nellie."

"He won't. He says she hasn't been gone forty-eight hours and as far as he knows, she may have killed Mike and gone on the lamb."

"That's ridiculous. Where would she go? Her whole world is here. Her home, her horses, her business. She didn't kill Mike, and she certainly wouldn't disappear and make us all worry about her like this," I declared.

"We gotta do something," Charlie said. "I'm gonna go talk to some of the boys. We'll put together a search party. Maybe she went on a walk to clear her head and got hurt. She could be out in the woods lost and injured without food."

"Are you sure you're up to it?" I asked. Charlie was still flushed and agitated. Hiking around in the woods for hours wouldn't help his blood pressure.

Charlie shrugged off my concerns. "I'm fine. I'm just angrier than a rattlesnake in a room full of rocking chairs. Me and the boys are going to find Nellie, and when we do, I'm going to tell Clint what for!" Charlie jammed his cap on his head and walked with a determined air out of my office.

I sighed. Charlie and his boys were all in their late sixties and seventies. Although most of them were fairly spry for their age and a few of them had served in Vietnam and knew their way around the woods, I still worried. What if someone had Nellie? They might bumble their way in and get hurt. Dang it, Clint. Why did he have to be so bullheaded?

Since I couldn't leave work and join in the search, I decided to do some online searching. I had looked into Mike's background but hadn't ferreted out any information on Nellie. I opened up our library databases and began a search on Nellie and her family.

A half an hour later, I was startled away from the computer screen when Wade knocked on my door.

"What's on the agenda for today, boss?" Wade asked. Despite the trauma he'd experienced during his time in the service which included the loss of his lower legs, Wade stayed upbeat and had a strong work ethic. My sister had a keeper as far as I was concerned.

"Nellie's missing. Charlie's out looking for her. Something's hinky with Darcy and her crew, and I've got a raging headache from looking at this computer screen for too long."

"Whoa. Rewind to the part about Nellie missing."

I told Wade everything from this morning starting with my conversation with Willow after the yoga class and ending with Charlie leaving to go on a search mission for Nellie.

"Charlie's a stand-up guy. I appreciate him wanting to go find Nellie, but he might not be the best candidate to traipse around the woods to find her. What makes him think she's lost or hurt?"

"Honestly, I think he wants to be doing something useful, and it was the only thing he could think to do. Clint says for all he knows, Nellie could have killed Mike and made a run for it."

"Do you think he really believes that or is he being stubborn?"

"Stubborn. Clint loves Nellie as much as the rest of us do. I guarantee you he's looking for her and not because he believes she killed Mike."

"Good. I'd hate to go knock some sense into him," Wade cracked his knuckles.

"I think the law frowns on assaulting an officer."

"I'll slip."

"You and my sister. Comedians. I found out some information online this morning, so my headache was not in vain. Turns out Nellie was cleared of all charges related to Mike's money laundering. Her family are all fishermen and gator hunters who have no ties to the Cajun mafia. Her only crime was marrying too young to know any better. Mike testified that Nellie was completely in the dark when it came to his criminal misdeeds."

"That's good. Anything else?" Wade asked.

"Glad you asked. Our protesters are pretty hardcore when it comes to going after factories and businesses that harm the environment. I went back over newspaper articles from the last couple of years. Our girl, Darcy, is a career protester. The weird thing? I found no trace of her before three years ago. Either her name's not Darcy or something happened to cause her to go G.I. Jane radical."

"I doubt her real name is Darcy as much as I doubt Dragonfly and Moonflower are the other women's given names. How am I going to find out who they really are unless they tell me?" I threw up my hands in frustration. I wish people came with a book. It would come with their entire life history, their likes and dislikes, and anything else you needed to know about them. Life would be so much simpler.

"Phee, Phee, Phee," Wade said, shaking his head sadly. "Did they teach you nothing in library school?"

"Again with the comedy. Are you going to help me or am I going to have to make your work late on your date night with my sister?"

"I'm wounded!" Wade clutched at his chest. "All you need is a picture of their face and you can dump it into any of the big engines image search. Google, Facebook, all of them are doing it now. The world is a much smaller place than it was even five years ago."

"Really? And you people mock me because I refuse to go on social media. Who's the smart one? Me. My business is not out there in the ether for all the world to see. Juliet was going to do some digging into the protestors. I'm going to text her and get her to take some pictures. We'll see what we can find out."

"Good idea. In the meantime, I have books to check in and my adoring fan base to push books upon."

"I think since you're here, I'm going to go to lunch. I'm starving, and it may help my headache go away."

"Sounds like a plan, Stan," Wade said. "Pick me up a sandwich on your way back?"

"Will do." I grabbed my purse and jacket and headed out to track down a sandwich.

I ended up walking the few blocks to the Quickie Cow. It had the best jalapeno burgers in town and would serve peach shakes for another week before switching to pumpkin for the fall season. I picked up my order and a cold turkey sub for Wade and sat at one of the umbrella-topped tables near the woods. I unwrapped the burger and got ready to take the first bite of the hot, tasty concoction when Clint slid in next to me.

I set down my sandwich and glared at him.

"I don't want to talk to you," I said and picked up my tray to move to another table.

"I need to talk to you," Clint said, putting a hand out to stop me. "I don't have much time and I'm under a lot of pressure. Could you cut me a little slack?"

I sighed and sat back down. "What do you want?"

"I agree with you that something's going on with Nellie's disappearance. Agent Shields is breathing down my neck and she has Jaime doing cartwheels. You came to see me this morning to tell me something, didn't you?"

"I did. Willow overheard Darcy and Dragonfly talking. Darcy said something about not meaning to shove Mike and it was an accident. According to Willow, Darcy claimed Mike was rubbing his head and cursing at her when she left the factory."

"She didn't say anything about getting into an altercation with Mike when we questioned her earlier. She said she talked to him and he told her he wasn't dumping anything into the river."

"I thought it was something you needed to know," I said. "And for the record, I didn't poke my nose into anything. Willow stopped me at the end of yoga class and said I would know what to do. Well, her spirit guides said I would know which is pretty much the same thing."

"I appreciate that," Clint said. He grabbed my hand. "Listen, about the other night, I was a jerk and you're right to be angry with me. I've been doing nothing but working on this case and thinking about you. I want to talk to you about what's going on in my head, but right now with this murder and the federal agent…it's not the right time. But I promise you, when this is over, we'll sit down and we'll talk. A real talk."

"I can wait," I said softly. Clint wasn't one to open up and bare his soul. If he had finally decided to tell me what was going on with him, I could wait a little bit longer. "I'm not a fan of Agent Shields."

"Believe it or not, neither am I. Unfortunately, she can't get that into her head," Clint said. He took a napkin and wiped my mouth gently.

"Quickie Cow does have the best jalapeno burgers," I joked.

"I know, but unfortunately, I made an excuse to Agent Shields on why I needed to take a break from digging through Mike's financials. As far as she knows, I'm home giving Watson some kind of doggie medicine. I wanted to check on you and give you an update on Nellie. I sent Deputy Thompson by her house after Charlie came in, but he didn't find anything. We don't have probable cause to go inside, but from the outside, nothing was disturbed. For all we know, she took the day off to clear her head and went fishing."

"You don't really believe that, do you?"

"No. Nellie is the most responsible woman I know. If she told Charlie to pick her up, she would be there or call him to cancel. She isn't going to just disappear without telling anyone. I've got a call to her family to see if they've heard from her. With her son stationed on a carrier and her daughter-in-law visiting family in Montana, it's hard getting in touch with them. The son is trying to arrange transport home for Mike's funeral, but it may take a week before he gets here."

"Keep me posted?" I asked.

"Definitely. And Phee, I'm asking you to trust me when it comes to this investigation. Something big is going on with the pickle factory. I can't quite put my finger on it, but I will. I don't want to have to worry about you while I figure it out. Okay?"

"I know. I've been warned, and I'm taking it seriously."

He gave me a swift kiss and left. As I sat there finishing my burger and slurping my peach shake, I realized I hadn't told him about the note I received. Clint wasn't the only one who wanted me to keep my nose out of Nellie and Mike's business.

# CHAPTER EIGHTEEN

When I got back to the library, I was greeted by two eager faces. Juliet was waiting with Wade for me to get back from lunch. I handed Wade his sandwich.

"You took forever," Juliet said with a pout. "I've been waiting ages. I want to show you what Wade and I found with the image search."

"I was only gone forty-five minutes," I said. "Clint came to talk to me."

"I know," Wade and Juliet said at the same time then laughed.

"I told him you'd gone on a mission to find food. With only two places to grab lunch, even someone without a background in tracking down suspects could find you," Wade said.

"So what does Mr. Law and Disorder want?" Juliet said in a snarky tone.

"He's looking into Nellie's disappearance but on the down low. There's something weird going on with this whole mess. He pretty much admitted that he's having to be at Agent Shield's beck and call. Jaime is bending over backwards to cooperate with her. Clint sent Deputy Thompson out to look around her house, but he didn't find anything. They're waiting on a call back from her family."

"Maybe she got a call that something happened to family back home in Louisiana and took off without letting anyone know," Wade suggested.

"How?" I asked. "No car, remember?"

"Show her what we found with the image search," Wade

said to Juliet. He offered her a bite of his lunch, but she wrinkled her nose at the onions and ketchup oozing from the bun.

"It's a big clue. Monumental even." Juliet said, unable to keep the excitement from her voice. "You really can find anything on the internet."

"You're scaring me," I said. I vowed to stay off any form of social media for the foreseeable future.

Juliet clicked a few keys on her laptop then turned it around for me to see. I saw dozens of images of Darcy on the screen. Most of them showed her in the company of Dragonfly and Moonflower, but a few shots were older images that looked like mugshots. I snatched the laptop out of Juliet's hands and clicked on one of the pictures.

"Wendy Foye was arrested last night for assaulting a night watchman at the Sloane Research Facility in Mercy Park. Foye, age 35, permanent residence unknown, assaulted James Cormac when he attempted to stop the suspect from opening cages containing research subjects.

The suspect broke a back window and was spotted by Cormac as she used wire cutters to open cages. When Cormac approached Foye, she began to beat him on his head. Cormac was able to contain the suspect and place her in a large cage. He then called for police. Bail has been set at twenty-five thousand dollars." I finished reading the article. "Holy crime capers! I guess she's not as anti-violence as she claims which makes what Willow overheard even more concerning."

"Exactly what I thought. Here's the best part." Juliet reached over and clicked on one of the other photographs. "She jumped bail and is still on the run."

"That was over ten years ago," I said as my eyes skimmed the article. "Surely the statute of limitations has run."

"Oh, contraire, mon frère." Juliet wiggled her finger at me. "I mean, mon souer, my sister, whatever. I knew I should have taken French in high school. Once you've been charged and jump bail, the statute of limitations is null and void. The statute of limitations is only if they haven't brought charges. She was charged."

"How'd you get so smart?" I said, amazed at her knowledge of the law.

"I've been watching *Law & Order*. I was burnt out on the seventies cop shows, so I've updated my viewing list."

"It's cop shop talk every night at our house, Phee. You created a monster." Wade rolled his eyes. "I ask to watch MMA or maybe a nice documentary even, and I get the eyes. You know the look I'm talking about it. The look that could slice tomatoes and not even blink."

"You love it when I practice putting on the handcuffs. Admit it." Juliet kissed Wade.

"Yuck and double yuck," I said. "Too much information for me. I need to bleach my ears now."

"I'm still thinking about going to school to be a police officer," Juliet said. "I haven't made up my mind, but in the meantime, I'm learning it all through prime time television. It's the American way."

"Heaven help us all. Did you talk to Darcy or the other protesters? Anything about a confrontation with Mike?"

"I didn't get a chance. I got your text and started snapping pictures of everyone. Darcy started acting kind of weird after that, so I hotfooted it out of there and gave the pictures to Wade."

"Should we tell Agent Shields what we found? I think wanted fugitives do fall under the FBI, not local police," Wade said.

"I don't like Agent Shields, so my vote is no. The FBI will find out eventually," Juliet said.

"I'll call Lu. She might hate us poking into the investigation, but she'll be glad to get the information. She's not a fan of Agent Shields either," I said.

"She can join our Anti-Shields fan club," Juliet said. "I'll even make t-shirts. We'll hold meetings."

"Nice," I laughed. "I'll bring the snacks."

"I will let you book nerds get back to your book shuffling or whatever it is you people do," Juliet closed her laptop and put it in her backpack. She hugged Wade and left.

"I'm calling Lu," I said. "Will you hold down the fort for a little bit longer?"

"I live to serve, boss lady."

"Glad to hear it." I shut my office door and dialed Lu's cell phone number. She picked up on the second ring. "Lu, can you talk?"

"Give me a second to walk outside where I have better service, Mom," Lu said. A moment later, she came back on the line. "What's going on, Phee?"

"Mom?"

"I wasn't alone. As low woman on the deputy totem pole, I don't need any hassle from the sheriff or anyone else," Lu said.

"I found out some interesting information about our protester, Darcy. Her real name is Wendy Foye, and she's a fugitive from Massachusetts."

"Wow! That is news. She didn't trip our radar at all when we questioned everyone about Mike. Thanks for the tip. I could definitely use some brownie points with the feds right now."

"Why is everyone so on edge about Agent Shields and the FBI?" I asked. I couldn't believe cool, confident Lu would let anyone shake her.

"Mike wasn't who everyone thought he was," Lu said in a low voice.

"Yeah, I know. I'm the one who dug up the information about his links to the Cajun mafia."

"No. It's something more than that. Clint and I think there is something bigger going on to get the feds to come to Miller's Cove to investigate a former wise guy who runs a pickle factory. Agent Shields isn't sharing, and I don't like it. Secrets are how people get killed."

"Be careful," I said. "And Lu?"

"Yeah?"

"Keep an eye on Clint. Keep him safe for me. Okay?"

"You can count on it." She disconnected.

I was officially worried.

# CHAPTER NINETEEN

It was busy the rest of the afternoon. Our morning volunteer left, and Wade taught an Internet for Seniors class which left me manning the circulation desk.

"I'm trying to find a book, Phee. I know it used to be here, but I can't find it," Mrs. Crandall said. Her face puckered into a frustrated mass of wrinkles. Seventy years old, Mrs. Crandall refused to read any books released in the past decade. As far as she was concerned, all new books were fluff and nonsense.

"It might be checked out," I replied. "Did you check the catalog?"

"Certainly. I couldn't find an entry for it. I know it's here. I read it five years ago."

"It might have been weeded from the collection."

"Weeded? What? Young lady, this is a library, not a garden. Now, help me find the book," Mrs. Crandall demanded.

"Mrs. Crandall, when a book becomes worn or hasn't been checked out in quite some time, it gets weeded from the collection. In other words, it's permanently deleted."

"That's ridiculous! Why would you do that? I'm a taxpayer, and I pay good money for the books here in the library. The books should remain on the shelves!" She pounded the floor with her cane.

"Ma'am, I understand you're upset. We only have so many shelves and so much space. We can't keep every book ever purchased. As the librarian, I have to make room for new books which means damaged or outdated books have to be deleted. I'm sorry, but it has to be done."

"It's a travesty! I'm going to the town council. Heads will roll!" Mrs. Crandall shouted with her cane raised in the air like a Viking giving a call to battle.

"You do what you feel you must," I said calmly.

I wasn't worried. She complained to the town council at least once a year about me weeding books. She gave me an evil glare before thumping out the front door.

"Time for you to get fired again, I see," Wade laughed. His class was over, and it was time to start shutting everything down before closing.

"I think it's funny. By this time tomorrow, she'll forget and come in for a different book," I replied.

"Patience of Job," Wade said.

"Not always. She's a regular patron, so I don't mind her complaints. It's the people who come in once a year and expect you to have every book their friends have in the New York Public Library. When you don't, they look at you like you grew a second head."

"Small town library. Small town collection. I like Miller's Cove, but it's not for everyone." Wade shrugged.

"We seem to have more big city problems creeping in every day. I don't know if we'll ever be able to go back to the way it was."

"I think Mike was killed by someone from outside of Miller's Cove. There's too much weird stuff going on related to his factory and his family ties. Has anyone talked to his nephew, Eddie?"

"Juliet and I spoke with him briefly outside the sheriff's office on Monday, but other than that, no."

"I think it's time I buy that man a beer and find out about his family and what he's actually doing here, don't you?" Wade shut down the computer.

"Aren't you the same guy wanting Juliet and me to lay low and not nose around the murder?"

"Meh!" He waved away my protest. "That was you and Juls. I'll be fine. I'll ask Anthony to go with me and call it a guys' night out. Eddie's the new guy in town so it would be perfectly natural for us to ask him if he wants to go."

"Have you even met the guy yet?" I asked.

"Sure. He goes and works out at the high school during open gym hours. I go to keep my boyish figure. He goes to become a bigger, hairier ape." Wade picked up his backpack and waved goodbye to me. "I'll let you know what I find out."

I shook my head in dismay. Wade's bravado would end up getting him into trouble. Hopefully, Anthony would keep them both level-headed.

I locked the door behind me. I was tired and emotionally wrung-out from the day. Nellie was missing. Clint was all over the place with our relationship. Why didn't I have a pair of ruby slippers like Dorothy where I could tap them together and make my hometown like it used to be? Since I didn't have ruby slippers, a bowl of chocolate chip cookie dough ice cream, warm pajamas and a good book would have to do.

An hour later, Fritz and Ferdie were fed, and I was in my favorite Eeyore pajamas with Piglet slippers. I scooped some ice cream into a bowl and shuffled my way to the living room. Settling onto my chaise lounge, I snuggled under my lap quilt and opened up my book to read.

I awoke to the sound of Fritz barking. I rubbed my eyes and realized I'd fallen asleep reading. What time was it? I realized that someone was knocking on my door. I wondered who could be here this late at night.

I untangled myself from my blanket and fumbled my way to the door. I peered through the glass and saw Anthony and

Wade grinning at me. I quickly unlocked the door.

"What in the world are you two doing here?"

"We had drinks with Eddie and we got news," Wade slurred. "My best buddy, Anfunny, said we needed to tell you before we forgot."

"Yeah." Anthony slung his arm around Wade's shoulder. "His best buddy, Anthony. Oh, wait. That's me."

"Shhh…" I shushed them. "You two monkeys get inside."

"We're monkeys!" Anthony snickered. "Ooo! Ooo!"

I ushered them inside the house and into the kitchen. I made them sit at the kitchen table while I started a pot of coffee.

"How did you two get here?" I asked. They better not have driven a car in their current state.

"We walked from the restaurant," Wade said. "Well, he walked and I rolled." He pointed to his wheelchair.

"I gather you two were able to find Eddie and invite him out for a drink."

"Yeah," Anthony said. "We learned a lot, too. Not a little. A lot."

"A lot," Wade repeated. "For such a big dude, he cannot hold his alcohol. Three drinks and he was singing like a…like a…"

"A bufferfly!" Anthony interjected. "He sang like a bufferfly! Get it? Because Eddie's buff. Oh, never mind."

I poured them both a cup of coffee and made them drink it before I tried to find out anything else. "So what did you learn?"

"He said the pickle factory wasn't only Mike's. Eddie said it's a family-owned business. He came up to learn the business," Anthony said. "Eddie suggested some cost-cutting moves. How much you want to bet that one of those moves was dumping the brine into the streams?"

"Did he admit to it?" I asked. With Mike's love of fishing, it hadn't made sense that he would dump in the streams.

"Not exactly, but I would bet my piggy bank that Eddie was the one behind it."

"Tell her about the girl," Wade motioned to Anthony.

"Girl?" I asked.

"Eddie's got a woman here in town. Somebody from back home," Anthony whispered.

"Who?"

"We don't know, but she's hot," Wade hissed. "Don't tell Juliet I said that because she'll be mad."

"I won't say a word." I patted his hand.

"I love your sister," Wade said and hung his head. "I'm going to marry her one day and make her a dishonest woman."

"That's nice. Have another cup of coffee." I turned back to Anthony. "Any clue at all who the woman might be?"

"Not sure, but Eddie said she's like a Barbie doll." His hands demonstrated a curvaceous woman.

"That's not a big help. So he's dating a woman with boobs and a butt. I don't think we could really call that a clue, do you?"

"It's what he said. Eddie said she was like a Barbie doll, whatever that means."

"You boys did a good job investigating. Now it's time to get you boys to bed and let you sleep off all that hard work. Wade, you sleep in the downstairs guest room. Anthony, I'm going to put you on the couch."

"You're gonna be a great sister," Wade grinned. "I get to fight crime and read books with you. I love your sister. I'm gonna marry her one day."

"I know," I said. I tugged Wade up from the chair and

guided him to my spare bedroom. I pulled some blankets and a pillow out of my linen closet and made up the couch for Anthony.

"I appreciate the couch, Phee," Anthony said. "I didn't try to go toe-to-toe on the drinking like Wade did, but I held my own. Definitely not in any shape to drive back to the lake."

"It's not a problem," I reassured himself. "Goodnight."

Even though their methods were not condoned by Nancy Drew or Hercule Poirot, I had to admit Wade and Anthony had found out some valuable information. Mike may not have been the one behind the dumping and there was another connection to Louisiana – Eddie's girlfriend. On that thought, I crawled into bed and decided that I would sort it out in the morning after a good night's sleep.

# CHAPTER TWENTY

Juliet's voice disrupted my dream. I reluctantly left the coliseum-sized library filled with solely with mysteries by my favorite authors and awoke to the smell of coffee and voices in my kitchen. I looked at the clock on my nightstand and saw it was only a little past six a.m. Why was my life cursed by early risers? The only redeeming factor? My sister had finally learned how to make coffee in my percolator so I was guaranteed a decent caffeine fix.

I slipped my feet into my Piglet slippers and scuffed my way to the kitchen. The sight of Clint, Lu, Wade, Juliet and Anthony crowded around my kitchen table greeted me.

"Girl, I thought you were exaggerating about your eyebrow at the diner." Lu whistled. "You look like you were attacked by a weed whacker."

"Only if the weed whacker is a blonde witch in a blue suit. If I wasn't such a sweet and forgiving person, I would seek revenge in a most heinous and hairy fashion. I am rising above and letting it go," I said with a self-righteous sniff. "I need caffeine and quick."

Juliet shoved a cup into my hand and gave me the chair next to Clint. She sat down on Wade's lap. I don't think I had ever had so many people in my kitchen at one time. I needed to finish painting my dining room soon if I was going to start hosting impromptu six a.m. coffee klatches.

I took several large sips of coffee. I gave the sweet nectar of the gods (or goddesses according to Juliet) a moment to clear the morning fuzz from my brain. Sighing with pleasure, I looked around at everyone. "So why do I have everyone here at the crack of dawn?"

"Wade didn't come home," Juliet said as if that answered it all.

"And?" I asked.

"I called Lu to put out an all-points bulletin on him since I knew he and Anthony went to talk to Eddie."

"Despite the fact I asked you to stay out of it," Clint pointed out.

"Technically, you asked Phee and Juliet to stay out of it. You didn't say anything about me or Anthony," Wade said. Clint shot him a baleful look. Wade held his hands up. "I'm just an innocent bystander trying to stay in the good graces of my hot girlfriend and the woman who signs my paycheck."

"Somehow I doubt you protest too much when Holmes and Watson here drag you into these things," Clint said.

"I called Anthony's cell phone this morning, and he didn't answer. He hadn't answered when I called last night for our planned phone date. Lu Gifford does not get stood up. Ever. I patrolled all of the possible places they could drink in the county and found Anthony's car parked downtown." Lu explained. "By this time, Clint was out walking Watson. I picked him up, and we figured we'd come by here to see if you'd heard from them."

"And I was coming to wake you up since you didn't answer the phone," Juliet said. "It kept going straight to voicemail."

"It's probably dead. I forgot to charge it yesterday. Why didn't you call the house phone?"

"I didn't think of it. Who has a phone in their house anymore now that we all have cell phones?"

"Me. Well, now that the whole Scooby gang is here, can we please talk about the case?" I held up my hand to stop Clint before he had a chance to protest. "Stop. I already know what you're going to say. Everyone here knows that you are wasting your time and your breath. Besides, Juliet and I kick butt when it comes to clue cracking and interrogating suspects. They are more at ease with us, two innocent-looking women just having a casual conversation, then when they are under the spotlight glare of the law."

"I didn't create the monster," Juliet said. "I only throw mystery books and chocolate under the door when she gets like this."

"I give up. I feel like I'm outnumbered on all sides and out of bullets," Clint said in defeat. "I'll discuss the case on one condition."

"What's that?" I asked.

"I'm starving. What do you have to eat in this place?"

I got up and peered in my refrigerator. Fortunately, I had a dozen eggs and some bacon. My bread box yielded a loaf of bread. Anthony volunteered to cook while we shared what we knew so far.

"Mike was killed on Sunday night or early Monday morning, correct?" Juliet said. She grabbed a notepad from her bag and started jotting things down.

"The full coroner's report came back yesterday. He died Sunday night between seven o'clock and midnight. They couldn't narrow the window because of the effect of the pickle brine on the body. All you need to know is there will not be an open casket at the funeral," Lu said.

"The official cause of death was drowning," Clint said, "but before that he received multiple blows to the back of the head. It would have rendered him unconscious."

"We know Darcy got into a confrontation with him and shoved him. Maybe her shove was actually a whack or two to the head," I suggested.

"Speaking of Darcy, formerly known as Wendy Foye, she is now in police custody awaiting extradition to Massachusetts. She refuses to saw a word to anyone, including her court-appointed attorney," Lu said. "I got brownie points with the sheriff for bringing her in. Thanks for the tip, Phee."

"I'm glad my sleuthing from the safety of my four library walls could help you out." I tried not to shoot a smug look at Clint but failed.

He put his arm around me and said, "Library sleuthing is fine. It's the breaking into houses and going to strip clubs that puts my teeth on edge. The doctor's going to put me on high blood pressure medication if I keep dating you."

"If not for my shenanigans, you would lead a very boring life as a deputy in this town. I keep you on your toes."

"You do," Clint admitted as he squeezed my knee under the table.

"We also know that Nellie went by the factory Sunday night but when she saw a red car she believed belonged to Dusty, she didn't stop," Juliet added.

"Darcy and Dragonfly were at the factory. Darcy previously admitted to meeting with Mike, but she said he got angry and she left. Darcy claimed she thought someone was in the factory with Mike and he acted strange, but she might be covering up the fact that she killed him," Lu said.

"Someone, possibly Mike, has been dumping pickle brine into the water causing a major fish kill. This made the protestors angry, but it might have pissed off some outdoorsmen from the area, too. It opens up a whole new realm of possible suspects," Clint said.

"Mike was having an affair with Dusty. She's a scorned lover because he won't leave Nellie," I added. "I think she's definitely a stronger suspect than Nellie."

"You say that because Nellie's your friend. You have to be objective," Anthony said. He slid a plate of eggs and bacon in front of me.

"I'm objective. I can objectively say without a doubt that Nellie didn't kill Mike. Affair or not, she loved him too much. He was the father of her child," I said.

"Eddie was at the factory, too," Juliet said.

"Nellie told me that he called her Sunday night to apologize for not making it out to the factory that night," I said. I took a bite of the eggs. They were perfectly scrambled. Anthony was definitely a chef extraordinaire as far as I was concerned.

"But remember Dragonfly said a big truck roared by them that night," Juliet reminded me. "Do we know anyone else in town with a big truck who would be at the factory?"

"Not really. Joe McAndrew has his tow truck, but I don't recall anyone else who works there driving a big truck," Wade said. "Most folks have little pickups or plain old work trucks. Nothing fancy like Eddie's monster."

"I think we might have to pull Eddie back into the office to talk to him again. According to him, he didn't see his uncle Sunday evening," Clint said.

"Good," I said. I finished off the last bit of eggs and toast on my plate.

"Anthony, these eggs are perfect and you cooked the bacon the way I like it. I need to get some tips from you," Wade said.

"It's all in the pan, man. All in the pan," Anthony grinned. "I heard back from my guy at the EPA. Mike underwent a full inspection by the USDA inspectors less than six months ago. The factory undergoes regular inspections since they distribute food. They didn't find anything untoward at the time and the EPA didn't have a complaint registered about his factory until two months ago."

"What happened in the past six months that has Mike dating a pole dancing hussy and spoiling his beloved lake and forest?" I wondered.

"And why after thirty years together, would he throw away his wife and marriage?" Juliet asked.

"Some people don't realize what they have until they've lost or destroyed it," Clint said. He gave me a deep, searching look.

"Sometimes people think things are destroyed when they are only a little dinged up. Things can be fixed," I said, taking a sip of coffee and looking at everyone but Clint.

"Are we still talking about Mike's murder or something else?" Lu said, looking at me confused.

I chuckled and went back to eating my breakfast.

# CHAPTER TWENTY ONE

After everyone finished eating and helped clean up, the gang dispersed to head to their homes or work. Clint and Lu had an early morning meeting they remained close-lipped about despite my best attempts to pry the information out of them.

"I can't tell you, Phee. A great deal is at stake right now with the feds in town and Jaime practically having a coronary every time anyone even sneezes. All I can say is that some of the bad things you think only happen in big cities has snuck its way into our little backwoods town," Clint said. He leaned down and gave me a kiss. He stuck his hat on his head and turned to leave.

"Is this early morning meeting with Agent Shields?" I tried to keep the distaste for the woman out of my voice but failed.

"Phee, Agent Shields is the worst kind of federal agent. She's arrogant, thinks she knows more than those of us who grew up in this town, and to top it off, she thinks she is God's gift to men," Clint said. "I prefer my woman to love books, have weird taste in footwear and one eyebrow."

"Are you making fun of my Piglet slippers?" I arched my one eyebrow at him.

"Certainly not."

"Good. Because if you were, I was going to buy another pair in your size," I threatened. "Are you guys doing anything more to find Nellie?"

"Officially? No. Unofficially, I've got some of my buddies in the state police keeping an eye out. Deputy Thompson is looking into it on his off time, too."

"Thank you," I said. "I'm worried. Nellie wouldn't run off and disappear. It's not like her. Not even with all that's going on, she's a fighter. Plus, she hates change. Leaving Miller's Cove would be way too much change for her right now along with everything else."

"I know," Clint said. "I'm sorry, Phee. I have to go. I promised you we would talk, and we will. Right now…I…"

"I'm here. Go catch criminals and have your meeting. When all of this mess is settled, you and I will talk," I promised.

"I love you, Ophelia Jefferson. Don't you ever forget it," Clint said and with a tip of his hat, he walked out the door.

"That was so romantic," Juliet sniffed.

Startled, I jumped. "Eavesdropping, little sister?"

"Not really. I was coming to ask you to borrow a jacket. I left in a hurry this morning, and it's chilly outside."

I waved her towards my bedroom. "Borrow what you want. I don't know if any of my jackets will be long enough. I'm a hobbit in comparison to you."

"Hobbits are precious."

"What's on your agenda for today?" I asked. I reached down to scratch Fritz behind his ears.

"I'm teaching wheelchair yoga at the VA at nine and after that I'm free. My class at the senior center is cancelled today. The seniors are going on a field trip to a museum in Burlington."

"Pick me up after work?"

"Sure. What did you have in mind?"

"I want to go out to Nellie's house and have a look around," I said.

"I'm sure the house is locked."

"I have a key," I said slyly. "Nellie told me to keep it since

I go and feed the horses when she and Mike go out of town. They have a gazillion houseplants and I always water them."

"You are a resourceful girl, Phee Jefferson. Glad I have you in the family tree."

I gave an evil laugh. "You have no idea."

Promptly at closing, Juliet cruised up to the front of the library and honked. I hurried out the door and jumped in Ole Blue. She did an illegal u-turn and headed out of town to Nellie's farmette, which was a fancy realtor's term for a house with ten acres.

We pulled to the rear of the house so the car wouldn't be spotted from the road. No need to advertise our shenanigans. I unlocked the rear door and glanced around. The kitchen smelled like old garbage. The trash can was half-full. No dishes in the sink, but there was an unwashed coffee cup on the counter. Was she snatched in the early morning hours?

"Where's Rosie?" Juliet asked, pointing to the empty dog food bowl.

"Oh my gosh! I completely forgot about her! Rosie! Rosie! Come on, sweet girl," I whistled. A small whine came from the next room. I hurried down the hall and found Rosie huddled underneath the couch, her little nose peeking out. "Come on, baby. Auntie Phee's come to take care of you. I have some chow chow for you."

I jogged back to the kitchen and searched the cupboards until I found some kibble. Pouring some into the bowl, I returned to the living room and placed it a few feet from the couch. Rosie slowly crawled out and sniffed tentatively at the bowl. Hunger overtook her fright, and she started to eat. I stroked her tiny little head and made soothing noises.

"Nellie wouldn't have left Rosie behind," Juliet said from the doorway. "While you take care of her, I'm going to look around the house."

"Okay." I continued to stroke Rosie and calm her down. Eventually, her hunger satisfied, she allowed me to pick her up and go find Juliet.

"Look what I found." She held up a silver piece of metal.

"What is it?" I asked.

"I'm not sure, but it was in the hallway next to a toppled side table. I also found Nellie's purse. She definitely wouldn't have gone anywhere without it."

"Clint had Deputy Thompson come out here and check around the house, but he didn't come inside."

"Nellie's been taken. I'm positive she's in danger. We have to get Sheriff Dawes to take this seriously."

"I agree, but according to Clint and Lu, he's jumping through hoops to keep the feds happy. He'll pull out the standard party line of waiting forty-eight hours before filing a missing person's report."

"You're probably right. We've got to do something though. I can't stand thinking that Nellie's hurt or scared."

"Me either. There's more going on here than just Mike's murder. I think our next move will be to find out more about Dusty Rose. I'm sure she didn't spill her guts when she was questioned."

"I doubt she'll tell us much of anything." Juliet scratched Rosie on her head.

"I didn't say we were going to talk to her. We're going back to the Lamplighter," I said.

"Because that plan was so successful last time." Juliet shook her head.

"This time we're going in disguise. They'll never recognize us."

"If you say so."

"Trust me. I've got a plan. Let's go back to my house."

# CHAPTER TWENTY TWO

An hour and a half later, we pulled into the parking lot of the Lamplighter. I pulled out the compact from my purse and checked to make sure my disguise was still in place.

"I feel ridiculous," Juliet said. "This thing is making my face itch."

"It's only for a little bit longer. It's for Nellie." I stepped out of the car and adjusted my wig. Operation Pole Dancer Recon was in play. "Remember my name is Ralph Hutchins and you're John Wiggins. We're feed salesmen from Des Moines on our way back to Iowa from a big pig feed convention."

"I hope I don't have to pee," Juliet complained. "I have no magic to pull that act out of my hat."

"I'm glad I kept all the costumes from the Founder's Day play. Who knew Ben Franklin could be pimped out to look modern? A little haircut on the wig, a ball cap and a denim shirt and jeans…Bam! Instant man."

"I look ridiculous. This beard is over the top. I look like I'm Amish."

"You look like a feed salesman from Iowa. It's perfect. You only need to do one more thing to pull off this disguise."

"What's that?" Juliet asked.

"Lose the purse. It's a dead giveaway."

Juliet grabbed her keys out of her purse and tucked them into her jeans. She wore an old shirt of our grandfather's that had been packed away in a box waiting for my next trip to Goodwill. I adjusted her baseball cap and decided it was now or never.

We stepped inside, and I sidled up to where Bruce was tending bar again. In the deepest voice I could muster, I said, "Gimme whatever you got on tap."

"Sure thing. How about your friend?"

"John? You wanna a beer?"

"Uh, sure, Ralph. That'd be awesome." Juliet croaked.

I rolled my eyes at her. Feed salesmen didn't say awesome. "Me and my pal here were just at a pig feed convention."

"You don't say," Bruce said, bored. He slid two mugs of beer across the bar to me. I dug around in my front pocket and pulled out some money to pay.

"Yep. Got some new product coming out this fall that's going to make those hogs bacon-producing machines." I made a show of looking at the stage. Fortune shined upon me because it was Dusty dancing. "That sure is a nice-looking filly on stage. What's her name?"

"That's Dusty Rose. You got lucky. It's her last night here. She's moving back to Louisiana this week. Why don't you boys go and enjoy the show. Dusty will give you a private lap dance for the right price."

"I think I'll do that. Come on, John. Let's cop a squat close to the stage so I can check out that prime filet." I grabbed my beer and swaggered across the floor.

"You look and sound ridiculous," Juliet hissed.

"At least I didn't say that a beer would be awesome. Oh my god, were you trying to blow our cover?" I hissed back. I grabbed a chair next to the stage and sat down. I went to cross my legs, then thought twice about it. I leaned back and tried to sit like a man. Should I scratch something or would that be over the top?

Dusty strutted close to the edge and shook her rear end at us. I tried not to grimace. Hopefully, she would think it was a grin. I pulled a twenty out of my pocket and waved it at her. She winked at me and leaned down so I could put it in her G-string. When we found Nellie, she'd better give me free coffee for a year.

Dusty went back to the pole and swung around and around advertising her ample assets to the crowd. The song ended and she walked off the stage. A few minutes later, she came over to our table and simpered, "Is there anything a girl like me can do for two fine-looking gentleman like yourselves?"

"You sure can, darling. Why don't you set a spell and I'll buy you a drink. Would that be alright?" I asked. Thank goodness my reading habits included fifties detective novels with canned banter and cheap women.

"I'd like that. Let me go say hello to a couple of folks and I'll be right back." She walked away trailing her fingers across my shoulders.

"Oh my sweet milk of magnesia. I can't believe she didn't realize we're not dudes," Juliet said gleefully. "I'm going to be the best undercover cop ever!"

"Slow your roll, Serpico," I warned. "The night's still early. Thank goodness it's dark in here."

"Phee, guess who Dusty's chatting with right now," Juliet said. When I went to turn around, she grabbed my hand to stop me. "Don't turn around!"

"Dude," I said in a gruff voice. "Keep your hands off my dollar bills. Get your own." I glared at Juliet. Guys don't grab other guy's hands. She was going to let the cat out of the bag and we'd be done for the night.

"Sorry, Ralph. I thought it was my cash." Juliet coughed. "Darn cold is kicking my ass tonight. It ain't nothing that a hot looking woman couldn't cure."

"Nice," I whispered. "So who's she talking to?"

"Eddie. They are looking pretty darn chummy, too."

"I've got to check it out." I dropped a dollar on the floor. As I leaned down to pick it up, I peeked across the room. Dusty was sitting knee-to-knee with Eddie and the two appeared deep in conversation. "Those two are up to no good. Mark my words, they know each other and I don't mean as future aunt and nephew. I'm talking they know each other in a way that mating minks know each other."

"Ew," Juliet scowled. "Thanks for that visual. Fortunately, I don't wear fur."

"Buy a girl a drink, boys?"

A tall brunette stood in front of me with nothing on but a G-string and some glittered pasties. I gulped. "We were kind of waiting on Dusty. She promised us a private dance."

The brunette lifted her leg and straddled my lap. "Oh, you don't want Dusty. She's busy with her boyfriend. I could show you a real good time."

"Boyfriend?" I squeaked then cleared my throat and tried again. "That's her boyfriend? I thought she was seeing some old guy."

"Nah. She's been seeing this guy for months. I think they knew each other back in Louisiana. She's heading back there soon." She trailed her hands down my arm. "Now, how about Misty shows daddy how bad she can be."

Misty leaned down and placed her large breasts in my face and shimmied them. "Nope! Nope! Game over. Juliet, we gotta go." I shoved Misty away and jumped up from the chair.

"What the heck?" Misty frowned. "Wait a minute. You aren't a man. You're a woman. What kind of freak game are you playing?"

"No game. Just a bet with my friend here. Sorry for the inconvenience." I threw a twenty dollar bill at her and grabbed

Juliet. "Let's go."

Juliet took a last gulp of her beer and followed me out the door. Without another word, we ran out the door and hopped into Ole Blue. It wasn't until we were a mile down the road that Juliet burst into laughter. "Whooee, Ralph. You got yourself into a heap of trouble back there. Almost got yourself a private lap dance. I would pay good money for a picture of when she put her boobs in your face."

"Not funny," I said. "I'm going to have to sterilize my face. I don't think I'll ever drink milk again."

"Priceless. Absolutely priceless." Juliet was laughing so hard that tears were streaming down her face. "I can't wait to tell Wade."

"Oh no. You can't tell anyone about this. It needs to go in the vault and stay there until your deathbed."

"I can't keep this a secret. It's the best story ever. Rick is going to love to hear about this at Sunday dinner."

"No you don't! Mom and Dad would find out then and we would both be toast. I'm declaring sister pact."

"You wouldn't."

"I am." I crossed my arms. The sister pact was sacred. Once declared, Juliet and I were bound to secrecy.

"Oh crap on a cracker. Alright, Flea, but I'm putting this in my memoirs so be prepared."

"Fine. Five year moratorium on the retelling."

"You rain on more of my parades," Juliet pouted.

"I guess our instincts about Dusty were right," I said. "I knew she was up to something. She and Eddie are a couple. She's from Louisiana. Eddie told Wade and Anthony his girlfriend is from back home. Misty said he was her boyfriend. Two plus two definitely equals four here."

"It's a little disturbing, don't you think?"

"What?" I peeled my fake mustache off and removed my wig. My long hair fell down around my shoulders and I combed my fingers through it.

"Think about it. Dusty Rose was seeing Mike and Eddie."

"I see what you mean. I think there's something else going on here. Mike may not have been Mister Personality and he might have given you the creeps, but he adored Nellie. I'm still having a hard time with the idea of him cheating on Nellie."

"You may be right," Juliet agreed. "You know what I want?"

"What?"

"A hot shower and to pull this Abe Lincoln beard from my face!"

# CHAPTER TWENTY THREE

Despite Juliet's pleas that we shower and change clothes first, I made her head to the sheriff's office. Since it was almost nine o'clock, I assumed we would have to talk to one of the part-time deputies on night duty. I was surprised to see Clint's and Lu's vehicles still parked next to the building. No wonder they both seemed on edge. With twelve plus hour shifts, it had to be taking a toll on the department.

Angie, the night clerk, manned the desk. She was a recent graduate from high school and an avid reader. "Miss Jefferson, did you come here looking for my overdue library book? I promise I'll turn it in tomorrow. I'm on the last chapter." She held up an urban fantasy to show me.

"No, Juliet and I have something to tell Clint and Lu about Mike's murder. Their cars are in the parking lot. Are they here or out on a case?"

"Is that your sister Juliet next to you? Did you two go to a costume party?" Angie asked, her mouth open as she took in Juliet's disguise.

"Something like that," I answered. I wasn't going to get into it with Angie. Thank goodness I had taken my wig and mustache off in the car. "Can I head on back?"

Without really waiting for an answer, I opened the glass door that connected the front reception area to the offices in back. Juliet scurried after me before Angie could stop us. I peeked into Clint and Lu's shared office, but didn't see them. Heading to the conference room, I spotted Clint.

"Clint," I called out to catch his attention. "I've got to talk to you. It's important."

Startled, Clint looked up. "Hey, Phee. Juliet? Is that you? What in the blue blazes are you doing dressed like a man?"

"I'm exploring my masculine side, Clint." Juliet said dryly. "Your girlfriend. My sister. Need I say more?"

Lu peeked around the doorframe. "Juliet, you make a hunk of a man. I want to butter you and sop you up with a biscuit." She cackled.

"I've got to tell you what we discovered today. I went by Nellie's house and…" Before I could finish, Agent Shields stepped out of the conference room.

"Miss Jefferson." She nodded at me. "I'm assuming this is the other Miss Jefferson, but I don't want to be politically incorrect."

Juliet yanked at the beard she had attached with spirit gum earlier in the evening. It peeled away leaving her face red. "I'm Juliet. Phee's sister. We met before."

"Oh, right. So what have you two amateurs screwed up now?"

A slow burn roiled in my stomach and worked its way up to my head. I had had enough of Agent Shields with her oh-so-federal blue suits and long blonde hair. I wanted to rip out both her eyebrows as payback. I was so angry. I sputtered and couldn't get the words out.

"Hold on a minute, Shields. Phee and Juliet have given us valuable information on cases in the past. They are both a part of Jaime's neighborhood watch initiative. Why don't we hear what they have to say?" Clint interjected.

"I don't know what kind of mom and pop cop shop you yokels are running here, but I will not have these two mess up an investigation that I've been working for a year. Why don't you two ladies go home and bake some cookies or whatever you small town types do.”

“Enough!” Clint roared and slammed his fist against the doorframe. “Agent Shields, we have jumped through hoops to cooperate with you, but you will not ever speak to the woman I love and her sister like that again. You want to talk amateur? You have behaved with a severe lack of professional courtesy and decorum. If you want any further assistance from me then you better back your attitude right out the door and leave it there. Do I make myself clear?”

“Yeah!” Lu cheered and did a little fist pump in the air.

“I’ll be talking to the sheriff about your outburst in the morning, Deputy,” she said, ice dripping from her words. “Any dream you ever entertained about joining the FBI just flew out the window.”

“Good riddance. I’m here to stay. If Jaime has a problem with me, he can have my badge and gun. I’ll be damned if you’ll treat Phee like this.” He grabbed his hat and slammed it on his head. “It’s been a long day. I need to get something to eat and get some sleep and so does my partner. I’m out of here.”

Juliet and I stood with our mouths hanging open. It took me a minute to realize he expected me to follow him. I darted after him with Juliet close on my heels.

“Wait a second,” Lu called. “I’m coming.”

We hurried after Clint as he stormed out the front doors. I gave Angie a quick wave. “Thanks, Angie. Don’t worry about the book.”

Clint stood on the sidewalk waiting for Juliet and me. “Damn the FBI and their superiority complex. I’ve had all I can take of Agent Shields.”

“Thanks for standing up for me.” I made a tentative move towards him. He pulled me into his arms and held me tightly to his chest.

"I'm an idiot. I've been a half-assed boyfriend and a half-assed human being lately."

"No argument from me," Juliet said. "What? I'm nothing if not honest."

"He has been a little bit of a jerk lately. I wanted to taser him, but I didn't want to fill out the paperwork in case it really hurt him," Lu said.

"Thanks for the comments from the peanut gallery," Clint said. "Sheesh. Tough crowd. Phee, you're awfully quiet."

"I'm still kind of awestruck that you told that evil woman to go to hell."

"Let's see if I have a job in the morning. I'm starving. Can we go grab a bite to eat and talk there?"

"Thank goodness because I'm so hungry I was chomping on sugar cubes in there," Lu said.

"I'm going to beg off and go home and shower. I have to get the rest of this beard gunk off of me. It's making my face itch. I'll talk to you in the morning, Phee."

"Sister pact," I warned her.

"Whatever." She got into Ole Blue and with a quick beep of her horn, she was gone.

I got into Clint's truck with him. We headed towards Quickie Cow since they were the only place still open. As we drove down Main Street, I saw the darkened interior of Nellie Jo's Cup o' Joe and a lump formed in my throat. I wondered where she was tonight. Was she scared? Hurt?

We pulled into Quickie Cow, and Lu pulled in next to us. I wasn't hungry, so I sat down at a picnic table and waited while Lu and Clint ordered. Ten minutes later, they both sat down carrying trays filled with burgers and mountains of French fries.

"I am so hungry I want to gnaw off my arm," Lu said

around a mouthful of fries. She took a sip of soda. "So I'm dying to know. Why was Juliet dressed like a dude?"

"We went back to the Lamplighter to find out more about Dusty." I didn't meet Clint's eyes.

Clint had been picking up his hamburger, but he set it back on his tray. "I thought I asked you not to go there? It isn't a place for nice girls like you and Juliet."

"Which is why we went in disguise as nice guys. I was Ralph, and Juliet was John. We were feed salesmen from Iowa," I explained.

"You dressed as a guy, too?" Lu guffawed. "Pictures! I want pictures!"

"Do you really think that made you any safer?" Clint asked.

Lu interrupted. "Shut the hell up, Clint."

"What?" Clint looked at her confused.

"You heard me. I feel like my partner is Tarzan. Me Tarzan. Phee Jane. What the hell? Phee is one of the smartest women I know. You don't give her credit, and you act like she's going to break anytime she steps foot out of that library of hers. Give it a rest."

"Thanks, Lu," I said.

"And you," Lu turned to me. "You let him do it. One minute you're Miss Super Librarian, then the minute he walks in the door, you turn into a simpering doormat."

"I…uh…I…okay," I stuttered. She was right. I lost all sense of who I was the minute Clint was around.

"Darn Skippy I'm right. But I don't want to talk about you two and your dysfunctional relationship right now. I'm hungry. I'm tired. I want to know what you found out."

"Okay." I blinked in surprise. Lu was a straight shooter even when it hurt. And it did hurt. A lot. I needed time to sort this out in my brain, but it wasn't the time or the place. Nellie needed me.

"Start at the beginning, Phee," Clint said gently. I think he was as shocked by Lu's outburst as I was. "You said at the station that you went to Nellie's."

"We went to Nellie's. I forgot I had a key to her place from when they would go out of town," I said, crossing my fingers under the table. It was only a tiny fib. "I water the houseplants and feed the horses for them. I'm sure something happened to Nellie and she didn't disappear on her own. She left Rosie behind."

"She would never leave Rosie. She's like a second child to her," Clint said.

"What the heck is a Rosie?" Lu interjected.

"Rosie is their most prized possession. She's a little teacup Chihuahua. They took her everywhere with them," I explained. "There was a side table knocked over in the hallway. We found this, too." I dug around in my bag and pulled out the piece of silver metal.

"What is it?" Lu asked.

Clint took it from me and held it up. "Looks like it goes on a belt or shoe. It's real silver. Could be unrelated to Nellie's disappearance, but I'll have the forensics team in Burlington look at it."

"Get to the good part," Lu prompted.

"I wanted to find more out about Dusty. I knew we couldn't go back to the bar because she'd recognize us. I had the costumes left from Founder's Day. I trimmed Ben Franklin's wig and use a little spirit gum and facial hair. Shazam! I'm a man."

Lu burst out laughing. A second later, a slow smile spread across Clint's face. "It's pretty funny."

"I make a very convincing man, thank you very much.

There's a new pig feed coming out that is going to knock your pig knuckles off."

Lu hooted so loudly it made me jump. Clint started to laugh. I had to admit that we probably looked ridiculous in our disguises. "Okay. I admit it was not my best idea, but we did find out something."

Clint got his laughter under control, and Lu had subsided into a few snorts and hiccups. I waited for them to take a drink of soda before I shared what we had discovered.

"Eddie was at the bar with his girlfriend," I said.

"So?" Clint asked.

"His girlfriend is Dusty Rose. If she and Eddie haven't been in cahoots all along, I'll eat my fake mustache!"

# CHAPTER TWENTY FOUR

Clint and Lu finished eating. Lu offered to give me a lift home since Clint's was in the opposite direction. I didn't hesitate to accept. Lu's "come to Jesus" speech as my dad called them had knocked me for a loop. I didn't like being a doormat, and I really didn't like that other people saw me that way.

Clint gave a disappointed look as I hopped in Lu's car. He leaned through the window and gave me a swift kiss on the cheek. "We still need to have that talk."

"We will when Nellie's been found and everything is back to normal," I said firmly. My priority was Nellie. Everything else could wait.

"I'll find her," Clint promised. "Lu, I'll see you in the morning."

"If we both still have jobs," Lu replied.

Ten minutes later I was home and giving Rosie, Fritz and Ferdinand lots of puppy and fat cat love. At least these guys didn't want more than a warm bed, a full tummy and a scratch behind the ears. Wouldn't life be grand if men were so uncomplicated.

I slipped a DVD into my player. It was a good night for an Alfred Hitchcock movie. I had to work in the morning, but since the library opened late tomorrow, I could sleep in. The opening scene to *Vertigo* came onscreen, and I settled under the blanket.

A half an hour later, I could barely keep my eyes open. *Vertigo* would have to wait for another day. I put on my pink pig pajamas and crawled under the covers.

I dreamt of a sunny day in the park taking Fritz to play. Someone was standing over by the trees. The sun was glinting off something shiny at their feet. Frightened, but oddly compelled to find out more, I walked over to the figure. It was Eddie Johnson. I looked down at his feet and realized the sun had been shining on his boots with their fancy gator skin and bright silver toe guards.

I startled myself awake. Toe guard. That was what the shiny piece of metal in Nellie's house was. I remembered earlier this week when we met Eddie. He stepped out of his big truck and the sun glinted off the silver on his boots.

I grabbed my phone and called Juliet. It rang and rang. I pushed redial.

"Do you know what time it is?" Juliet groaned.

"Time for us to save Nellie. I think I know who has her."

"Who?"

"Eddie. The silver piece of metal we found at her house. It's from his boots. It's a silver toe guard they put on cowboy boots."

"You're right." Juliet sounded fully awake now. "But he's her family. He could have lost that toe guard when he visited Mike and Nellie."

"True," I said. I thought hard trying to come up with an argument to convince Clint and Lu to search Eddie's place for Nellie. "We have to tell the sheriff so they can pull him in for questioning. Clint agreed with me that Eddie and Dusty are sketchy characters. I guarantee that one or both of them have something to do with Nellie's disappearance."

"Stop by first thing in the morning before Agent Shields has had a chance to talk to the sheriff. Maybe if they find Nellie, they'll get a pass on last night's little confrontation," Juliet suggested. I heard her stifle a yawn.

"I have to work tomorrow. Can you call Lu first thing and convince her to bring Eddie in for more questioning?"

"I'll try. There isn't anything we can do right now. It's the middle of the night. It's strictly conjecture on our part that they have her. For all we know the Cajun mafia came up and snatched her to keep her quiet."

"True. The mafia would have been stealthy, too. Eddie has been seen in and around town. If he's the criminal, he's not keeping a very low profile."

"It's still worth checking out, Phee. I promise I'll call Lu first thing in the morning. By then, it will be forty-eight hours since Nellie disappeared, so they'll have to start officially looking for her. Try to get some sleep. I'll talk to you tomorrow."

I closed my eyes and tried to fall asleep. My mind whirled with all the possible scenarios involving Mike's murder, Nellie's disappearance, and Agent Shield's presence in town. The possibilities were endless. Finally, I drifted off to sleep. My dreams were filled with tiny Chihuahuas and Nellie tied to a chair and crying.

The next morning, I awoke tired from the restless night of tossing and turning from bad dreams. I took care of Rosie and Fritz. I gave Ferdie extra kibble with the agreement that he wouldn't terrorize the dogs while I was at work. Filling a to-go mug with coffee, I headed to work.

Saturday was always a busy day at the library. Parents who worked during the week brought their children for our Saturday story hour. We also hosted Science Saturdays with experiments and hands-on demonstrations for the older kids. Fortunately, I had an excellent group of community volunteers on Saturday who were always happy to help with the programs.

At one o'clock, I was cleaning up a gravity experiment involving marbles when Willow came in. She wasn't wearing her usual peaceful expression. She looked worried. Perhaps the spirits had sent her a warning.

"Hi, Willow."

"Phee," she said with a relieved smile. "You were just the person I needed to see."

"Need a book recommendation?" I asked.

"Nothing quite so easy," Willow said with a weak smile. "I want you to talk to Darcy."

"Darcy? Isn't she in jail awaiting extradition to Massachusetts?"

"Yes. She refuses to say a word to anyone, and the sheriff is trying to pin Mike's murder on her now. I was hoping you could go with me and get her to explain what happened Sunday night at the factory. I know Darcy. She may be a radical when it comes to protesting factories, but she's not a killer. The spirits told me to come to you, and you would help."

"Well, if the spirit guides said it, then it must be true." I tried to keep the sarcasm from my voice, but from Willow's hurt expression, I must not have succeeded. I sighed. "I'll go, but for all you know, she may have killed Mike. Maybe it was an accident, but she still could have killed him."

"Please come with me," Willow pleaded. "I know you'll make this right."

"She still has to return to face what she did years ago at the research facility," I said.

"I know."

"I have to work until three. Come back then and we'll walk over to the sheriff's. You're assuming Jaime will let us back into the holding cells to talk to her."

Willow grinned. "I knew you would say yes, so it's already

arranged."

Willow left after checking out some New Age titles on crystals and chakras I had ordered with her in mind. I didn't think Darcy would talk to me, but if it would set Willow's mind at ease, I would do it. Willow might be odd, but since her arrival in Miller's Cove during the artists' retreat, we had become friends. I still didn't believe that the stones spoke to her, but she was spot on sometimes with her words of wisdom.

At ten minutes to three, Willow came back with Dragonfly and Moonflower in tow. I hoped the sheriff wouldn't mind us coming *en masse* to visit Darcy. Jaime was like an uncle to me, so I knew he didn't care for people he considered "revolutionaries."

"Thanks for doing this, Phee," Dragonfly said. "I know you probably don't believe it, but Darcy is a good person. She gets a little…well, a little enthusiastic when it comes to her pet protests. She went too far one time, and it changed her whole life. She didn't mean to hurt the guard, and she's been trying to do the right thing ever since then. She never condones violence at any of her protests."

"Yeah. We're all about changing the world, not destroying it. The world includes all human beings even if some of them are jerks," Moonflower added.

I locked up, and we walked quickly over to the sheriff's office. There were three holding cells in the basement of the office. While access to sunlight was limited by small barred windows, Tina made sure prisoners, or as she liked to call them, temporary houseguests of the law, were well fed and had clean sheets and towels every day.

"Phee," Tina greeted me, "I see you brought friends with you. The sheriff said to let you talk to Darcy, but she has to stay in her cell."

"That's fine."

"Let me call Deputy Thompson from the back, and he'll talk you downstairs," Tina said, chomping on her ever-present piece of chewing gum.

Deputy Thompson took us down through the locked door to the downstairs until we stood outside of the one occupied cell. Darcy looked terrible. Although she was clean, her complexion was ashen, and her eyes were swollen from crying.

"Darcy," Dragonfly went to the bars and reached her hand through them.

"Ma'am," Deputy Thompson stepped forward and put a restraining hand on Dragonfly's arm. "You can't touch the prisoner."

"Sorry," Dragonfly said and pulled her hand back.

"Darcy," Willow said quietly. "I've brought Phee here to talk to you. The spirits said you would tell her what you know."

"The spirits were wrong," Darcy said and laid down on her cot, eyes closed.

"Wendy," I began, using her real name, "my friend, Nellie, is missing. I don't know what happened to you years ago, and I don't care. Nellie is a sweet and gentle soul who has nothing to do with fish kills, protests or anything else. If you don't want to help yourself, help Nellie. Tell us about Mike and if you know where she is, now's the time to say something."

"I don't know anything about Nellie," Darcy said, not opening her eyes.

"Dang it! My friend could be hurt and you want to play political prisoner. How does that fit in with your love the world attitude? Guess you only want to help some people. I'm out of here," I turned away from the cell to leave.

"Wait."

I turned back and waited. Darcy sat up and looked at me.

"I don't know anything about Nellie. I promise. If I did, I would tell you."

"What really happened between you and Mike?" I asked.

"I talked to him on Sunday like I told you before. He kept denying that he was dumping anything into the water. Mike swore he loved nature. He claimed he didn't know what I was talking about. He was acting weird and kept looking over his shoulder. I felt like he was ignoring me and I lost it."

"Lost it? What did you do, Darcy?" Moonflower asked. She looked scared for her friend.

"I pushed him," Darcy said in a small voice. "I was so angry. So tired of these factories and companies ruining our earth without a thought for the future. He hit his head on the door frame, but he didn't lose consciousness or anything. He was fine, but maybe he had a concussion. I'm sorry. I've let everyone down. All my talk about peaceful protesting, and I lose my temper and blow it."

"Ma'am, where were you and Mike when this happened?" Deputy Thompson had remained quiet during Darcy's confession, but now, he stepped forward to hear her response.

"In his office. Why?" Darcy asked.

"Mike was found in one of his pickle vats in the back of the factory. Nowhere near his office. Are you sure you're telling us everything?"

"I swear when I left he was standing up and rubbing the back of his head. He was cursing me and calling me a dirty hippie, but he was fine. We were nowhere near the factory floor. We were in the front part of the building by the offices and reception area."

"She was only inside for about fifteen minutes," Dragonfly interjected. "Not nearly enough time to kill him, drag him to the factory floor and stuff him in a vat."

"I didn't kill him?" Darcy sniffed and wiped her eyes.

"If you're telling the truth, no," Deputy Thompson said. "I'll pass this information on to the sheriff. You could have saved us some time and gotten us looking harder at another suspect if you had been honest from the start."

"I'm sorry," Darcy said. "All I ever wanted to do was help save the world from the bad guys."

"Did you see anything or hear anything else while you were there?" I asked.

"I might be mistaken, but I swear I heard a woman's voice. I thought maybe that's why Mike kept looking over his shoulder. I heard he had some woman on the side, and I assumed he was trying to hide the fact that his mistress was there."

"Thank you, Darcy. You may not have saved the world today, but you might just have saved Nellie." I hurried up the stairs leaving Willow, Dragonfly and Moonflower to finish visiting with Darcy. I had to talk to Clint or Lu about my dream and Darcy. Eddie and Dusty Rose were buried up to her fake boobs in Mike's murder, and they had to be stopped.

Lu was in her office when I came up the stairs. I sat down in one of her uncomfortable office chairs and told her about Darcy's confession.

When I was finished, Lu said, "It's probably a good thing Clint's bringing in Eddie and Dusty right now. I'm waiting for him to haul them both down to the station so we can interrogate them separately. Juliet called me early this morning and told me about the toe guard. We'll have to question Eddie on how he came to lose it in Nellie's house."

I was relieved there was a chance we might get to the bottom of Mike's murder and Nellie's disappearance. "I guess my trip to the Lamplighter accomplished something. You guys are taking a hard look at Eddie and Dusty as possible murder suspects."

"Actually, that's not why we're picking them up for questioning," Lu said. She typed something into her laptop. She waited a moment and whatever she read seemed to satisfy her. She turned back to me. "Eddie Johnson has been using the factory as a junction for his smuggling business."

"Smuggling? Like pirates?" I said, confused.

"Sort of. The Cajun mafia is tied up in all sorts of illegal operations - laundering money, smuggling weapons, shipping untaxed cigarettes and alcohol across state lines and into Canada. If it's a money-making scheme that skirts or actually jumps into the criminal realm, Eddie Johnson and his family are into it."

"Holy guacamole!" I exclaimed. This was happening in Miller's Cove? I couldn't imagine that level of criminal activity going on right under everyone's noses. "How long were they doing it? Was Mike in on it? Did Nellie know?"

"Hold your horses and your questions, Phee," Lu held up her hands in defense. "We don't know who else is involved. Agent Shields has been tracking the guns that Eddie's been smuggling for a few months. It finally led her to Miller's Cove and Mike's pickle factory. That's what she's been here investigating. If she can tie Eddie and his cronies to the gun shipments coming through the factory, then they'll go to jail for a long time."

"No wonder you guys have been on edge." Now it made sense why Clint and Lu had been working ridiculously long hours and were pushing for me to stay out of Mike's murder.

"Yeah, well, it's not like she told us what was going on at first. She made us think it was money laundering. I guess she's trying to make a name for herself with the agency. Now that we're bringing him in, it won't be a big hushed up investigation anymore. You still need to keep this information to yourself until the sheriff makes an arrest and does his press conference."

"Mum's my motto," I said and made a zipping motion across my lips. "I won't breathe a word to anyone. I hope they'll tell you where Nellie is."

"I do, too," Lu agreed. "I have ways of making people talk. If they have her, I'll get it out of them even if I have to use bamboo shoots under their nails."

I let Lu get back to work and headed towards the town's only garage to pick up Velma. Although I enjoyed walking in the cool temperatures of fall, I would be glad to have my beloved van back. I paid the bill which put a serious dent in my savings account and climbed in. I took a minute to rub my hands over her steering wheel and pat her dash. "Time to go home, Velma." I turned the key and she purred to life. I was back in the VW van saddle again.

I drove by Juliet and Wade's house to tell her the news. Lu's admonition to keep things to myself surely didn't include Juliet and Wade. We were all part of the crime-fighting team. I patted myself on the back for realizing there was something off about Eddie and Dusty right from the start.

I saw Clint coming towards me in his cruiser. Since there were no cars behind me, I slowed to a stop and rolled down my window as he came along the side of me. No one was in the backseat.

"I thought you were going to get Eddie and Dusty to bring them in for questioning," I said. "I talked to Lu. She told me that's where you were."

"Nothing's secret in this town," Clint sighed. "Agent Shields, the sheriff and I went to Dusty's trailer on the outskirts of town. The place was empty, and it looked like someone was in a hurry to leave. We found evidence that Eddie had been staying there, but he's long gone, too."

"Any sign of Nellie?" I asked hopefully.

"There was a chair with bits of duct tape on the arms and legs. We think they were holding her hostage in the back bedroom. Best we can tell they took her with them. I didn't find any blood at the scene or anything to indicate she was injured."

"Poor Nellie! Why aren't you out there looking for them?" I demanded.

"The FBI is handling it," Clint said. "We've been asked to stand down. It's a kidnapping case, and they have jurisdiction."

"If people had listened to me two days ago, they might have rescued her already," I said bitterly.

"I'm sorry, Phee. My hands are tied."

A car horn honked behind me. I rolled up my window without saying goodbye and drove away. I wanted to cry. What would happen to Nellie? Were they planning on taking her back to Louisiana and feed her to the alligators?

It was with a heavy heart that I pulled up in front of Juliet's house. When she opened up the door and saw the look on my face, she tugged me inside and pulled me into a big hug. "What's wrong, PheePhee?"

The words spilled out of me as I told her everything that had happened throughout the course of the day. "And now, they are probably on the run back to Louisiana. Once they get deep into the swamps, it will take an army to track them down," I finished with a weary sigh.

"They'll find her, Phee," Wade said from the doorway where he'd been listening. He had his legs back, and the wheelchair sat folded in the corner. "You may not like Agent

Shields, but I have a feeling she's a bloodhound when it comes to tracking down fugitives. She won't quit until she's caught them."

"I hope you're right."

"Come into the kitchen and have a glass of wine. The pasta sauce is almost done," Juliet said. She walked through the curved archway that separated the living room from the kitchen.

"I couldn't eat a thing. My stomach is tied up in knots worrying about Nellie."

"You need to eat. Starving yourself won't bring Nellie back any faster. This is one time I have to agree with Clint. Leave it to the professionals. The FBI knows how to track fugitives," Juliet said. She handed me a glass of red wine.

I sat down at the round wooden table. I took a sip of wine. "Lu came down on Clint and me last night. She said I was a doormat when it came to him. Do you think that's true?"

Juliet stayed silent and continued to stir the sauce in the pan with a wooden spoon. After a moment, she said, "Kind of."

"What? Really? A doormat? I think I'm stronger than that," I protested.

"In every other area of your life, yes. When it comes to him, you lose all sense of who you are. You act like that man makes the moon rise in the sky. He doesn't, Phee. He's a man. An ordinary man with personal demons that you might not be able to accept."

"I love him," I said simply.

"Sometimes, love isn't enough. Until he figures out what's going on in his head and his heart, he's not good for you. You, my dear sister, are sunshine and happiness wrapped up in a five foot two package. He's like a dense fog that's rolled in and covered it up. He's changed and not all of it is good change."

"You think it's because of me?"

"No. I think something's happened that he's not sharing with anyone, and it's eating him up inside. He loves family, or at least I always thought he did. You remember what he was like when we were kids. He spent every spare moment he could at our house. It was because he wanted to be part of a family. This declaration that he never wants one is baloney. Something else is up with that man." Juliet set the spoon down and turned off the stove. "Wade, dinner's ready."

Wade came in and grabbed three plates from the cupboard. He filled a plate with pasta and covered it with sauce. He put it in front of me. It smelled delicious. I guess I actually was hungry.

After dinner, Juliet suggested we go get an ice cream cone from the little shop down by the lake before it closed for the winter. Wade volunteered to stay behind and wash up.

"Not that I don't like ice cream, but all this domesticity is making me lose my figure." He patted his flat stomach. "Go ahead without me and by the time you get back, this kitchen will be sparkling. The Marines made sure I knew how to make everything spotless."

"Thank goodness because Juls is a slob," I said.

"Hey!" Juliet protested. "I resemble that remark!"

We took Velma since I wanted to break her back in after our short hiatus from each other. I swung by my house and let Fritz and Rosie out for their evening jaunt around the yard. After leaving them with some kibbles and a promise to be home in less than an hour, we were back on the road to the lake.

There was a long line at Carlotta's Ice Cream since all the locals wanted the last taste of summer in a crunchy cake cone before the stand closed for the season. As we stood in line, we overheard several people talking about Mike's murder and speculating on who could have killed him. Fortunately, no one believe Nellie could have, but Mrs. McGuire who checked out books from the occult and supernatural Dewey Decimal range claimed it was an alien assassination.

"You might not be a believer now, but wait until you wake up with their long fingers probing your nether regions and their big buggy eyes blazing into your very mind. Mark my words, Mike Johnson's murder was an alien assassination because they knew he was going to reveal that the source of his pickle recipe was Mars," Mrs. McGuire raved.

Juliet and I looked at each other and rolled our eyes. To think she had been our music teacher when we were in elementary school. We were next in line. We both ordered a swirl of chocolate and vanilla. We sat down in the grass cross-legged and licked our cones.

"Life doesn't get any better than this," I sighed. I licked a drip from my hand. "I don't want to ever leave Miller's Cove."

"Really?" Juliet asked. She bit the bottom of her cake cone and slurped out the dregs of her ice cream. "You never wanted to travel to Paris or London and see the world?"

"Not really. Too many bad guys and terrorists out there right now. I like it here where it's safe."

"It hasn't seemed very safe the past two years to me."

"Valid point," I conceded. "I want to raise a family here and have Mom and Dad babysit when I go on date night. I have the house, the dog, the cat and the picket fence. The only thing I don't have is a husband and two kids."

"Do you think Clint will ever change his mind about marriage and a family?" Juliet asked.

I was silent as I thought about it. I watched the moms and dads pushing their children on the swings down by the lake, and the couples kissing on blankets. I wanted it so badly. The thought I might not ever have it left a bitter taste on my tongue.

"Maybe," I said as I popped the last bite of cone into my mouth. I crunched and swallowed. "He seems to be having a change of heart. He said he wants to talk. If he hasn't changed his mind, I've made up my mind that we're done. No more mooning over him. No more putting up with his brooding silences. No more of his kisses and hugs and…" I stopped as I thought about not having Clint in my life.

"It's the right thing to do, Phee. If it's to be, then it will be. If not, it won't."

"That is the least profound thing you have ever said."

"Thanks." Juliet stuck out her tongue at me. "Now come on. Let's get home. We have brunch with the parents tomorrow, and Mom's still on her health food kick. Thank goodness Wade feeds me or I'd be a skeleton by now."

"I don't have that trouble. I look at an apple and gain five pounds. I don't know how come all the good genes went to you."

"You got the brains, the great hair and the money sense," Juliet offered. "I just got the long legs and the ability to eat a horse and stay thin. I think the trade-offs are fair."

"Hmmm." I didn't agree, but I wasn't going to argue.

We got in Velma and started to chug our way back to town. As we came to the stop sign at Pine Forest Lane and Hemlock Grove Road, a beat up Toyota Camry that was more primer grey than red blew through the stop sign without slowing.

"Was that…?"

"It was!" Juliet shouted. "I'd recognize those fake boobs anywhere. That was Dusty Rose. Hit it, Phee!"

I stepped on the gas and followed Dusty. Her tail lights were barely visible in the distance. She must be going eighty miles per hour. Velma didn't stand a chance of going that fast without rattling apart, but she went fast enough for me to keep the car visible. After a few miles of following her, it was easy to figure out where she was going. There was only one thing this far out of town – the pickle factory.

When the chain link fence that surrounded the factory came into view, I killed Velma's lights and pulled over to the side of the road. I could see the Toyota pulling up to the factory and stopping. A moment later, the interior light came on briefly then went out.

"What are we going to do?" Juliet asked. "We need to call the sheriff's office."

"I know, but we don't have time to wait for them to get here. It's twenty minutes and they could be loading Nellie up and leaving for all we know."

"I'm calling Wade," Juliet said. She pulled out her phone and called him. "Wade. Phee and I are at the pickle factory. Dusty Rose drove here and we followed her. We're parked outside the gates right now."

I could hear Wade squawking on the other end of the line. I wasn't sure what he was saying, but from the look on Juliet's face, he wasn't happy we were here.

I grabbed the phone from her and said, "Wade, be quiet and listen. Call Lu and tell her what's going on. We won't go in, but Juliet and I are going to do a little recon and make sure they aren't leaving." I hung up before he could say anything else.

"Is this really a good idea?" Juliet said. "I mean, Eddie is a thug in the Cajun Mafia. Guys like that are called enforcers. They are all brawny and stuff. They bump people off for the godfather. For all we know, he's in the factory, too."

"We aren't going to confront her. We're just going to check out the perimeter and peek in the windows to see if we spot

Nellie." I opened the glove compartment. "Ta da! I'm even prepared. I have our Super Librarian and Super Yogi masks."

"You're a regular freakin' Girl Scout is what you are," Juliet said, but she took the mask and put it over her head. The cursive Y glittered in the moonlight.

Slipping on my mask, I gave her a thumbs up and slipped out of Velma. Juliet followed behind me as we skirted the edge of the fence and stuck to the shadows. I didn't see any other vehicles at the factory, so chances were Dusty was on her own.

As I came up to the building, I realized the windows were too tall for me to see inside. I tried hopping, but it was a good foot higher than me.

"Give me a boost," I whispered to Juliet.

She cupped her hands together, and I stepped up. Juliet groaned as she boosted me to the window. "Lay off the chocolate if you plan on any more crime fighting," she whispered.

I peered through the dirt-crusted windows. I saw something, but it was hard to tell who or what it was. I rubbed the window and looked again. It was Nellie. She was tied to a chair in one of the offices.

"I see Nellie!" I whispered. I moved back away from the window. The change in position caused Juliet to drop me. I landed in a heap on top of her. Her yelp of pain seemed to echo in the night.

We froze and waited. After a minute without a sound from inside, I stood up. I reached down to help Juliet up, but the look of fear on her face made me freeze. I felt something hard and cold against my back.

"Evenin' ladies. Nice of you to join us," Eddie said in his Louisiana drawl.

I turned slowly and came face-to-face with his gun.

# CHAPTER TWENTY FIVE

"Take off those masks. Ya'll look ridiculous," Eddie commanded.

I peeled my mask from my head and dropped it to the ground. Juliet did, too. I tried to keep from shaking, but the realization that we might die tonight hit home when I looked into Eddie's cold, flat eyes. He reminded me of an alligator, cold-blooded and predatory.

"We were curious to see how pickles are made," Juliet squeaked.

"Shut up and get inside," Eddie snapped. "I don't have time for you two tonight."

We stumbled in through the factory doors. Dusty, who had been busy stuffing duffel bags with money, looked up in surprise. "Where did they come from?"

"I found them snooping around outside. I'll take care of them when I take care of Aunt Nellie. What's two more bodies at this point?" Eddie shoved me into the office where Nellie was.

"Phee! Juliet!" Nellie gasped. "I told you to stay out it. Now look what's happened." She looked tired and slightly worn around the edges, but at least she was alive.

"Ah, Nellie, you know we couldn't let the best muffin baker go down for a crime Eddie and Dusty committed. Clint's on his way. He'll take care of these two jokers," I said with more bravado than I actually felt.

"Shut it!" Eddie barked. "Dusty, get over here and tie these two up. Put a gag in their mouths, too. I don't want to hear their lip."

Dusty scurried over and shoved me into a chair. She wrapped rope around my wrists and ankles and yanked it tight. It bit into my skin causing me to wince with pain. Juliet was next and although she tried to appear brave, the tears forming in her eyes gave her away.

Dusty put masking tape over our mouths in an attempt to gag us. "Guess you two aren't such big men after all. Like I didn't see through those cockamamie disguises. Feed salesmen from Iowa. I ain't no dummy just off the turnip farm, you know."

Eddie and Dusty went back to the other room. I could hear them arguing over the best way to haul the bags of money. I wiggled my jaw and the masking tape popped loose from my mouth.

"Nellie," I whispered, "are you okay?"

"I'm okay. Hungry and a little sore from rolling around in the bed of his pickup trussed up like a hog on butchering day, but other than that, I'm fine.

"Clint and Lu should be here any minute," I promised.

"I hope so because Eddie has plans to put us on ice and making us gator food once he gets back home to Louisiana. He's got a delivery truck ready to roll out back full of guns and who knows what else. My mama warned me thirty years ago that Mike's family was bad news, but I didn't listen."

"So Eddie killed Mike?"

"Yep. Whacked him on the head with a crowbar and dumped him into a pickle vat. I guess blood ain't thicker than water after all," Nellie said bitterly. "I'm sorry."

"You have nothing to be sorry about, Nellie. None of this is your fault," I said.

"I'm the one who put the note in your newspaper," Nellie

admitted. "I was trying to scare you away."

Juliet had managed to loosen the tape on her mouth, too. "Be quiet. They're coming back."

Eddie strolled in with a gun in one hand and a leash in the other. Attached to the leash was an alligator with a bejeweled collar around its neck. It didn't look full grown, but the sight of those sharp teeth grinning at us from its snout made me almost pee my pants.

"Meet Ethel," Eddie said. "This lovely lady is going to ride in the back with you all the way to Louisiana. If you're good, I might let you pet her."

I could only stare wide-eyed at the gator. Where was Clint? I cursed my foolish, impulsive, dangerous idea to nose around the factory. I was a librarian, not a super hero or crime fighter. If I made it out of this factory alive, I would only dig up dead ancestors from dusty books ever again. I would never investigate a murder again.

"Dusty! You got us all loaded?" Eddie shouted over his shoulder.

Dusty came in to the room sweaty and red-faced from exertion. "Yeah. Thanks for the help."

"Somebody had to check on the gator bait," Eddie replied. "Time to go. Aunt Nellie, I'm going to untie you. You make one false move, and I'll shoot you dead."

"Your mama should have beat your hind end when you were a boy. No respect for your family or your elders," Nellie spat.

"The only thing I respect is cash money. Family doesn't make the world go round, Aunt Nellie. Money does."

Nellie looked at Juliet and me. "Girls, I'm sorry you got mixed up in this mess with my no account nephew. I love you both for trying to help me."

Eddie snorted. "They should have kept their noses out of it." He untied Nellie and shoved her over to where Dusty stood with a gun. She waved it at Nellie. Nellie stumbled forward.

"Hold it right there!" Clint's voice echoed from the dark recesses of the factory.

Eddie jumped over to Nellie and grabbed her around the neck. He put the gun to her head and shouted into the dark recesses of the factory. "I don't think so. I'm going to leave here with Aunt Nellie and no one's going to stop me. I get one whiff of a cop and I'll shoot her."

Eddie had dropped Ethel's leash in the chaos. The gator ambled towards Juliet and me. I tried shoving my chair back, but it wouldn't move. I was going to die by gator bite tonight.

A shot rang out and Ethel turned her large snout towards the sound. "Get that gator under control, Eddie, or the next shot goes in her head!"

"Dusty! Get Ethel!"

"I hate that gator! Get her yourself."

Eddie pulled his gun away from Nellie's head and aimed it at Dusty. "I said get Ethel. Do it now, or you'll be her next snack."

Dusty glowered at Eddie, but did as she was told. She grabbed Ethel's leash and the gator turned away from us. "Happy now?"

"Sure am, darlin'. You know I love that gator as much as I love you." He leaned over and patted Ethel.

Clint stepped through the doorway. "Drop the gun, Eddie. You too, Dusty."

"I don't think so." Eddie shoved Nellie away from him and pulled the trigger.

I watched in horror as a bright red poppy of blood bloomed on Clint's chest. He dropped to the concrete floor and was still.

"Clint!" I screamed and tried to lunge forward despite the ropes.

Seconds later, Lu, Jaime, and a dozen FBI agents stormed through the door and started barking orders. Overwhelmed by the sheer number of guns pointed in their direction, Eddie and Dusty dropped their weapons to the ground and slowly raised their hands.

Lu dropped by Clint's side and pressed her hands against the wound in his chest. "You fool! Why didn't you wait for backup." I could hear her fear as she tried to administer first aid.

"Get an ambulance!" Jaime shouted.

"Somebody let me loose!" I cried.

One of the FBI agents cut the ropes from around my wrists and ankles. I ran to Clint. Kneeling down next to him, I cradled his head in my lap. "Don't you die on me Clint Mason! I didn't stalk you all these years for you to leave me now."

"It looks like it missed his heart," Lu tried to reassure me.

"I love you, Clint. Please don't leave me," I sobbed and laid my head against his bleeding chest.

"I love you, too, Flea," Clint whispered. His voice was weak, but he was conscious. "Never gonna let you go…"

He faded back to unconsciousness as the EMTs swarmed around him to transport him to the hospital. Juliet pulled me away from Clint so they could do their work. I collapsed into her arms and cried.

# CHAPTER TWENTY SIX

Jaime let me follow the ambulance to the hospital. He said he would take my statement later. "You go, Phee, and make sure that boy stays alive."

I hugged Jaime and with Juliet in tow, dashed out to Velma. The twenty mile drive to Burlington seemed to take forever. Finally, the bright lights of the hospital loomed in my windshield. I squealed into the emergency entrance and asked Juliet to park Velma. I ran into the lobby looking around for anyone who could tell me about Clint's condition.

A woman sitting at the information desk looked up at my wild-eyed entrance. "Can I help you, ma'am?"

"My boyfriend. He's a policeman. He's been shot. I need to…" I gasped, not able to articulate my fear and worry about Clint's condition.

"Take a breath, ma'am," the woman cautioned. "They brought Deputy Mason through here about ten minutes ago. They rushed him up to surgery. If you want to have a seat in the waiting area, as soon as he's out of surgery, someone will come talk to you."

"Thank you," I breathed. He was still alive.

"Does he have a next of kin we need to call?"

"I…no. We're his family. I mean, his aunt died a long time ago, and he's always been a part of the Jefferson family," I fumbled for the words. It wasn't exactly true, but I had no idea where Clint's mother was or if she was even still alive. I doubt anyone but Clint knew.

"That's fine. I'm sure the sheriff's department has the

information we need on file. Go ahead and sit down. It's probably going to be awhile. There's coffee and vending machines down that hallway." She indicated the hall opposite her.

Juliet came in and led me to the bank of chairs against the wall. "Wade's on his way. I've called Mom and Dad and Rick. They're coming, too."

"Juliet," I cried softly, "what if I lose him? What if my stupid antics just killed the man I've loved my whole life?"

"Shush. You haven't killed him. Eddie Johnson is the one who fired the gun. Not you. It could have happened the same way if you had been there or not. It's part of his job. Every person who puts on a badge and a gun knows the risks they face daily."

"But he wouldn't have been there if it hadn't been for me."

"He may not have, but it could have happened on another call with another criminal. You cannot beat yourself up over this one. Lu said she thought it got his shoulder and went straight through. That's a scratch to a tough guy like Clint. Heck, he and Rick got hurt worse wrecking their motorcycles doing stupid stunts."

"Maybe," I sniffed, unconvinced.

"Remember the time they made a jump out of a piece of plywood and some rocks?"

"Yeah. That was a dumb idea."

"It sure was. Rick knocked out his tooth when he landed and wrecked. I thought Mom would have a coronary on the spot. Those two yahoos wanted to go again despite all the blood and the tooth in the dirt."

"I remember." I smiled at the thought of Rick and Clint arguing with my mom that they were okay and could make the jump if she would leave them alone.

"He's a tough guy. Stubborn, too. He won't let a bullet stand in his way."

Mom and Dad arrived with Rick rushing in after them. Rick ran up to Juliet and me and pulled us into a bear hug. "When the phone rang and Wade said Clint had been shot saving you two from the mafia, I thought he was yanking my chain. I'm glad you two aren't hurt, but I swear I'm going to lock you both in the basement and not let you out if you ever pull a stupid stunt like this again!"

"You won't get any argument from me," Juliet promised. "When that gator sniffed my way, I saw my whole life gone in a bite."

"How's Clint?" Mom asked as she hugged me.

"In surgery. They'll let us know when he's out."

"Is that your blood or Clint's," Dad asked, worry etched in the tight lines around his face and mouth.

I looked down and saw my pants and shirt were covered in blood. "It's Clint's. I…"

"I already let Wade know to stop by your house and take care of the animals and grab some clothes," Juliet reassured me. "He'll be here soon, and you can clean up in the bathroom."

On cue, Wade came in carrying a bag. He grabbed Juliet and kissed her hard on the lips before turning to me. "I'm glad you're okay, but if you two ever pull a stunt like this again, I'm locking you both in the basement."

"You and Rick both," Juliet joked weakly. "You must share the same dinosaur DNA. Don't worry. I'm sticking to yoga and meditation from now on."

"Me, too," I promised.

I went down the hall to the bathroom to change. As I splashed cold water on my face, I gazed at my reflection in the mirror. I still had a trace of Clint's blood on my chin. I reached up with my finger and scrubbed it away with a furious gesture. I stuffed my bloodied clothes into the bag and pushed it into the trash can.

Returning to my family, we all sat down to wait for news. After what seemed ages, but was probably only an hour, a surgeon came through the double doors.

"Are you folks here about Clint Mason?" He asked as he pulled down his mask.

I jumped up. "Yes. Is he okay?"

"He's out of surgery and will be just fine. Sore, but he'll recover. It was a clean shot through his shoulder. He'll be on desk duty for a while, but he'll make a full recovery."

The horrible weight that had been crushing my chest lifted. I collapsed back onto the chair and cried in relief. Clint would be okay.

My dad shook the surgeon's hand and thanked him. "When can he have visitors?"

"I think later today will be fine. One person can go up now and sit with him. He's still coming out of anesthesia, but it's fine if someone is with him."

"You go, Phee," Rick said gently. "Be there when he wakes up."

I followed the surgeon to where Clint lay in a recovery room. Machines beeped and hissed all around him. He looked so pale and small in the hospital bed. Nothing like the strong man I knew and loved.

I reached over and grasped his hand. I closed my eyes and prayed he would be okay. The doctor might have said he would make a full recovery, but seeing him in that bed covered with bandages pushed those reassurances aside.

I sat there for hours and must have drifted to sleep. It had been a long and stressful night. I awoke to the nurse gently shaking me awake. I started and my eyes went to Clint's face. He was awake and watching me. "Hey there," I said softly.

"Hey there," Clint echoed. He smiled and tried to sit up. The pain made him wince, and he eased back down. "Help me sit up."

I looked at the nurse. "It's okay. Move slowly and watch your bandages," she said. She helped him sit up and raised the bed. After she finished checking his vitals, she left us alone.

"I'm sorry," I said simply.

"For what? You have nothing to be sorry about. I'm the one who should be apologizing. I got myself shot because I didn't wait for backup."

"I got myself captured because I didn't let law enforcement handle things."

"You've got a point," Clint conceded. "I knew Eddie and Dusty weren't your garden-variety criminals. I warned you, Phee. You're stubborn and nosy and…"

I stood up, tears filling my eyes. "I know. I'm sorry." I tried to leave, but he grabbed my hand.

"Let me finish. Your stubborn and nosy and you exasperate me to no end, but I love you. You're also smart and beautiful and you care about people. I'm a big, dumb cop who's lucky to have you in my life."

"I love you, too," I said softly and sat back down. "I should have listened to you. Nellie's safe and the bad guys are in jail though."

"True," Clint conceded. "If we're going to do this forever thing, we need to establish some ground rules. I can't go getting shot and you can't be kidnapped on a regular basis. Your parents can't handle the stress and neither can I."

"Forever thing?"

"Forever. I really am like a bear in a candy shop. Wanting to eat the candy and tearing things up and making  a mess of things in the process."

"I'm candy?"

"You are the sweetest person I've ever known, and I love you," Clint said. "I've been avoiding love my whole life and along comes this crazy redhead I've known since she was four feet tall with braces."

"That's me, right?"

He smiled and squeezed my hand. "Yes, that's you. I'm head over heels in love with you, but it's making me break every vow I ever made."

"What are you talking about?" I asked, confused.

"Do you know anything about my life before I moved to Miller's Cove?"

"No. I only know that your father is dead. No one will tell me anything about your mom."

"My mom," Clint said with a tinge of bitterness. "My mother was not a nice person. She drank and cheated on my dad for years. My father was a nice guy but weak. He ended up killing himself when I was a kid. Mom took off and I ended up in Miller's Cove. I saw what love does to a person. It broke my dad. I vowed to never let a woman hurt me the way my mom hurt him."

"I would never do that to you. I'm not that kind of person. Surely you realize that."

Clint was silent for a minute. "My brain realizes it, but sometimes the scared ten-year old kid who still lives in my head chimes in and says something different."

"I understand," I said, and I did. I couldn't imagine what my life would be like if I hadn't been born to the wonderful parents I had. "What can I do?"

"Be patient when that kid in my head makes me act like a jerk. I've been protecting my heart for so long it's going to take me awhile to break those bad habits."

"I can be patient," I promised.

"Be my forever girl?" Clint asked softly. His eyes filled with hope, but I could see fear, too.

"Always," I said and kissed him. "Get some sleep and I'll be here when you wake up."

"Thanks, Phee," he said as his eyes slowly closed.

"For what?"

"For loving me, warts and all."

# CHAPTER TWENTY SEVEN

A week later, Clint was home from the hospital and staying with me until he fully recovered. Watson had become fast friends with Fritz, and Rosie was safely back with Nellie. Ferdie ruled over them like a doting grandfather.

On Sunday, everyone came over for dinner. Since my kitchen wasn't big enough to hold everyone, we had set up plastic tables and chairs borrowed from the church and put them in my empty dining room.

Wade and Juliet brought a bottle of wine and an enchilada casserole. Anthony and Lu came with a large German chocolate cake. Rick and Carrie had left the toddler twins at her parents to have a few hours of adult time.

While I was setting the makeshift dining room table with plates and silverware, I heard a knock on my front door.

"I'll get it," Juliet offered.

A moment later, Nellie walked into the dining room. She gave me a hug and started to cry.

"Why are you crying, Nellie? I'm okay."

"I'm crying because you're my friend, and my worthless nephew almost killed you and Juliet." She wiped the tears from her eyes with the back of her hand. "I should have never asked you to get involved in the first place."

"Yes, you should have. You're like family. That's what families do for each other. Please stay for dinner."

"I couldn't impose." Nellie shook her head.

"It's not an imposition at all," Clint said. "I insist. Lu's supposed to give me an update on the case. I think we're all curious to find out what the heck was going on behind the scenes."

"Thank you, Clint." Nellie gave him a kiss on his scruffy, unshaved cheek.

We gathered together at the table. After everyone's plate was full and we'd said grace, Lu told us what happened after we left for the hospital.

"Eddie was as silent as a Sphynx once he was handcuffed, but Dusty Rose had diarrhea of the mouth. She sucks as a master criminal," Lu informed us. "Turns out, Eddie came up from Louisiana with her in tow to bring Mike back into the family business. Mike refused to play along at first. Eddie threatened to hurt you, Nellie, if he didn't."

"His side of the family always was trashy and violent. I knew he was a bad egg." Nellie shook her head.

"Eddie was laundering money through the factory and hiding guns in the crates of cucumbers coming here from down south. It was also Eddie that started dumping the fish brine into the river."

"I knew it!" I exclaimed. "I knew Mike wouldn't hurt the fish."

"He also wasn't having an affair with Dusty. Dusty stayed closed to Mike in order to keep an eye on him when Eddie wasn't around. Threats to harm you kept Mike in line."

"Why did they kill him then?" Anthony asked.

"Nellie accidentally found the paperwork where Eddie had paid for Dusty's implants out of the factory's business account. Nellie thought Mike had paid for them. Mike told Eddie he couldn't keep secrets any longer. He would rather go to jail for crimes he didn't commit then let you think he would ever cheat on you."

"He always was a gentleman," Nellie said. "I shouldn't have

doubted him. If I'd believed him, he would still be alive."

"Maybe not," Lu said. "Eddie had plans on moving the whole family up from Louisiana and taking over the factory. They kept getting busted by the cops back home, so they needed a new stomping ground. Mike would never have let that happen. Mike was an obstacle, and Eddie had to get rid of him."

"What about Darcy?" Juliet asked. "What's going to happen to her?"

"She'll have to stand trial for her assault all those years ago. Chances are she'll have to spend at least a year in jail. We aren't pressing charges against her for pushing Mike. She didn't really hurt him, but it did give Eddie the perfect opportunity to get rid of Mike and pin the murder on someone else."

"He is such a snake in the grass!" Juliet exclaimed.

"You aren't kidding," Wade said. "I can't believe he was going to let an alligator eat you."

"What happened to Ethel, by the way?" I asked. It's not like I wanted to visit her at the gator pound or anything, but I wanted to make sure she wasn't chomping her way through Miller's Cove.

"Ethel is safely ensconced in the zoo at Burlington. I think she's happier, too. No more collar and leash. She is doing what gators do and liking it," Lu said.

"What is it gators do besides try to eat librarians?" I asked.

"They eat fish and sleep in the sun. That's the extent of my alligator trivia," Wade said.

"And all I really need to know. I don't plan on ever getting that up close and personal with one again," Juliet added.

"So the case is done?" Anthony asked. "Miller's Cove is back to normal. No more Cajun mafia?"

"They're all done. With the information we received from

Dusty, the FBI was able to coordinate raids in Louisiana and Texas. Any activity here in Miller's Cove was strictly Eddie."

"Thank goodness. I couldn't stand to think that those no-good swamp critters had followed me and Mike up here," Nellie burst out. "Mike and I left after he got himself out of that heap of mess that sent him to prison in the first place. I won't lie to you. I never asked where the money came from that helped us start over. Maybe I should have. We wanted a fresh start, and we built a good life together. I'm gonna miss his sorry butt." She wiped away a tear.

"He was a good man, Nellie," Clint said and put his arm around her. "He gave his life trying to keep you safe. You couldn't ask for a stronger love than he had for you."

"Speaking of men giving their lives for women they love." Lu gave an exaggerated cough. "I got stuck filling out the mountains of paperwork because somebody didn't wait for backup and went and got themselves shot. You owe me for the next year."

"A man's gotta do, what a man's gotta do." Clint shrugged. "My woman was in danger, and I would die to keep her safe."

"That's a full-time job with my sister. Actually, it's a full-time job with both my sisters. I always thought I was the adventurous one in the family. Clearly, I was mistaken," Rick said.

"It's okay, honey," Carrie patted Rick's shoulder. "We have all the adventure we need with two toddlers running wild through the house."

"True."

"No more Agent Shields?" I asked Lu.

"Nope. She's gone back to her office in D.C."

"Dang it."

"You aren't sorry to see her go, are you?" Juliet gave me a

puzzled look. "She was a first class rhymes with itch."

"No, but I am sorry I never had a chance to pay her back for what she did to my eyebrow." I lifted up my bangs and showed everyone. "I have at least another month of unibrow duty before my eyebrow fully recovers."

"I paid her back for you," Lu said with an evil grin. "I found a way into her room at the bed and breakfast. She should have played nicely with the locals." Lu pulled out her phone and showed us a picture. "Doesn't she look professional with purple hair?"

We burst out laughing. After that, we finished eating the amazing enchilada casserole and settled into conversations about things unrelated to crime. Anthony cut the cake, and Lu passed pieces around to everyone.

Wade stood up with a glass of wine in his hand. He raised it high and said, "I want to make a toast. There is nothing better in life than good food, good friends who are like family, and a good woman by your side."

"Here! Here!" Rick agreed.

"I'm not done." Wade set his glass down on the table and reached into his pocket. He pulled out a small box and a collective gasp went around the table. "Juliet, I can't get down on one knee because my bionic legs don't work like that. Would you do me the honor of one day when the moon is full and the stars are aligned and Willow's spirit guides say the time is right, marry me and be my love from now until the end of time?"

"Yes," Juliet whispered, her hands clasped to her chest.

"Did she say yes?" Wade looked around at us all in confusion.

"Yes, Wade Weaver, I will stand under the moon and the stars with you and declare you my true love forever."

For updates on forthcoming books, go to www.amyelilly.com

Join Phee, Juliet and Willow in Sedona, Arizona, for the next mystery in the Phee Jefferson series, **Browsing for Trouble** (December 2016).

**Phee is browsing for trouble wherever she goes.**

A gorgeous spa in a beautiful locale, a girls' weekend…murder. Phee and Juliet are having the time of their lives at Sedona's Sunrise Spa and Retreat. After an outdoor sunrise yoga session, they head to the spa where they discover a body buried in the mud bath. Phee's relaxing vacation quickly turns into a hunt for a killer. Phee is always browsing for trouble wherever she goes.

Coming in Late Summer 2016

# Death Kicked the Milk Bucket

# CHAPTER ONE

Claire stomped out of the building. Unfortunately, her attempt to slam the door failed miserably. It eased shut slowly and closed with a soft whoosh of air. The large, overstuffed tote bag filled with ten years of her career slipped off her shoulder. She struggled to carry it all to her old Subaru parked in the company parking lot. As she yanked the tote bag up, the strap ripped and everything tumbled to the pavement.

"Dang it! If one more bad thing happens, I swear I won't be responsible for my actions." Claire declared to the empty lot. Sighing, she bent down to gather up her belongings. She heard a tearing sound as her pencil skirt split up the back. "Really? You've got to be kidding me. I guess that's what I get for challenging the universe." Claire finished gathering up her files and desk knickknacks and stuffed them back into her tote. She grabbed it around the bottom and made her way to her car. Claire fumbled around in her purse to find her keys and gave a triumphant "ha" when she yanked them from the detritus of her purse. When she popped open the trunk, Claire heard a tiny mew coming from the dumpster. As she slammed the trunk shut, another small meow sounded. Claire walked to the dumpster and peered inside. Nestled in a small cardboard box surrounded by garbage and rotting food was a tiny orange kitten. It looked up at her and let out another meow.

"Poor little thing. Are you hungry? Somebody must have dumped you here and left you to fend for yourself." Claire reached into the dumpster, lifted the fluffy orange kitten and snuggled him to her chest. It immediately started purring. "Well, you and I are just having a bad day. I got thrown out like trash, too. Would you like to come home with me?" As if it understood her, the kitten meowed and purred louder. Laughing, Claire picked carried the kitten to her car. She pulled a t-shirt from her gym bag, settled the furry bundle on to the passenger seat, then headed to her apartment.

Once home, Claire poured a small bowl of milk for the kitten. "I guess you need a name. How about Gingersnap?" Claire sat down on the kitchen floor and gently stroked the kitten's back. "You can be Ginger for short." Claire's cellphone buzzed on the counter. She struggled up from the floor to answer. Isabella's name appeared on the screen, and Claire hit the answer button.

"Hey, woman! How was your day?" Isabella asked cheerfully. In the background, Claire could hear the children laughing and yelling. "Knock it off you little monsters! I'm trying to talk to Claire and I can't hear over your screeching." After years of friendship, Claire was used to Isabella carrying on multiple conversations while on the phone.

"I got fired," Claire responded glumly.

"Oh my gosh, Claire! What happened?" Isabella asked in a shocked voice. "Kids, please be quiet!. Go play in your room until dinner's ready. Matthew quit hitting your brother. Sorry. They're out of control with their dad out of town this week. So tell me everything."

"Nothing happened. Mr. Simpson called me into his office and started going on and on about the economic downturn and how sacrifices needed to be made...blah blah blah. Five minutes later, I am in HR signing papers. Before the ink was dry, a security guard told me that I had one hour to pack my desk and leave the building. Ten years on the job and I'm kicked to the curb like two-day old fish. It wasn't just me either. There were two other people let go today." Claire slumped onto her overstuffed couch, kicked off her heels and put her feet up on the coffee table.

"I am so sorry. What are you going to do?" Isabella asked.

"No clue. I don't even want to think about it tonight. I'll worry about it tomorrow. Darrin is supposed to take me out tonight. He called this morning and said he needed to see me. Maybe he's finally going to pop the question. He's been very secretive lately. I'm pretty sure he's been ring shopping. I'll be Mrs. Stanislowski. Wife of Dr. Stanislowski." Claire let the name roll off her lips. "It sounds kind of posh."

"If you say so," Isabella grunted. She was not a fan of Darrin. In her opinion, he was boring and uptight. "Well, I've got to get dinner ready before the kids eat the dog. Text me when you get home tonight."

"Will do. Bye." Claire disconnected and pulled herself up from the couch. Darrin was going to be there to pick her up soon, so she needed to hurry and get ready. He hated to be kept waiting. She pulled off her now ruined skirt and kicked it next to her hamper. Slipping off her stockings and silk blouse, Claire rummaged around in her closet for something slinky and sophisticated to wear. She chose a deep turquoise dress with a scoop neck and slipped it over her head. She quickly pulled her hair into a French twist and freshened her makeup. She added a pair of tear drop silver earrings and slipped her feet into her favorite black peekaboo toe heels. As she was spritzing on perfume, a knock sounded on her door.

Claire hurried to the door to let Darrin in. "Hi, sweetheart. Right on time. I just need to grab my purse, and I'll be ready to go."

"Claire, I'd like to talk to you," Darrin walked in and shut the door behind him.

"Uh...okay? You sound serious. Let's go into the living room." Claire thought he must be nervous and wanted to ask her in private. Darrin wasn't a fan of public displays of affection. She sat down on the couch. Instead of sitting next to her, Darrin sat in the chair. "What did you want to talk about?" She gave him an encouraging smile.

"This isn't easy for me. We've been seeing each other for a while now." Darrin cleared his throat and swallowed. "And Claire, it's just...I've been seeing somebody else." He looked everywhere but at her.

Shocked, Claire struggled to grasp what he had just told her. "How long?"

"Does that really matter? I mean, what matters is that you and I aren't a good fit. You should just accept that it's over." Darrin finished stiffly. He started to stand up.

"No. No, I don't think so. You don't come in here and out of the blue tell me you've been seeing someone else and then walk out the door. I'm sorry, but I deserve an explanation. No. Scratch that. I demand an answer. We've been seeing each other for almost a year. I have gone to all of your boring functions. I've been nice to your mother which is no easy feat, let me tell you. That woman is a dragon from hell. I've smiled and schmoozed everyone you told me to schmooze even when they were busy grabbing my butt the minute your back was turned. So, you, Darrin Stanislowski, owe me a freakin' explanation!" Claire's voice had risen in volume. She was so upset she was trembling.

"It's not you, Claire. You've been great. You are great. You and I together as a couple are not so great," Darrin said calmly. His lack of emotion angered Claire. She felt her ears get hot.

"Really? It's not me? How could it not be me? You are dumping me on what has already been a horrible day! I deserve an explanation!" Claire demanded angrily.

"I'm gay. Okay. Are you happy?" Darrin yelled back at her. His words immediately dampened her anger. "I'm tired of hiding who I am. I'm tired of using you to hide it. You deserve better. I knew you were expecting a marriage proposal soon. It's not like you've been subtle. I don't want to live a lie anymore. I'm planning on telling my friends and family, but I felt you deserved to hear it from me first. I'm sorry, Claire. I didn't mean to hurt you." Darrin's unhappiness filled the room.

"Wait. You're gay. Really?" Claire was trying to process what he had just told her. "Are you actually seeing someone or did you just say that to make it easier for me to hate you?" She was trying to wrap her brain around the idea of the man she had been seeing for the past year wasn't who she thought he was.

"I've met someone. He's made me realize that I don't have to live a lie. You would like him, Claire. He's funny and smart. He makes me happy. I want someone to make you happy like that, too." He gave her a sad smile. "I am so sorry that I've been lying to you. I hope you'll forgive me and we can be friends."

"I just...I don't know. I mean, I'm just not understanding how I didn't realize. Listen, can you just go now? I want to be by myself. I need to be alone. So please, just go." Claire wiped the angry tears that had started to fall with the back of her hand.

"I understand. Claire, I really am sorry." Darrin tried to give her a hug, but Claire shrugged him off. He walked out of the apartment and shut the door quietly behind him.

Once he was gone, Claire sat back down on the sofa and leaned her head back as she tried to accept what she just heard. Her boyfriend of a year had just dumped her for a guy. She got laid off from the only job she had ever held. She had less than a month's worth of savings in the bank and a fifteen-year-old Subaru that was a crap shoot every day on whether it would start. Claire felt a tickle on her cheek. She turned her head to see Ginger sniffing her. She reached up and stroked the kitten's fuzzy head. "Well, Ginger, looks like we've only got each other, girl. What are we going to do?" Ginger leaped down on to Claire's lap and curled up to go to sleep. "You've got exactly the right idea, girl." Claire kicked off her shoes and settled back onto the couch to figure out her next move.

Claire awoke to kitten whiskers tickling her chin. She gave Gingersnap a quick pat on the head and put her on the ground. A quick glance at the clock and Claire realized she had slept through the night. It was early morning and the sun was just peeking up over the city's skyline. She went into her small kitchen and started a pot of coffee. She popped a bagel in the toaster and searched through her fridge for cream cheese. Her refrigerator shelves revealed a limp bunch of carrots next to a jar of olives but nothing else. She settled on strawberry jam. Smearing the bagel with a large dollop of jam and pouring a cup of coffee, Claire sat on the bar stool at her kitchen counter. She opened her laptop and began to search the online help wanted ads. "Hmmmm...let's see if we can find someplace looking for an out-of-work history major whose only experience is writing advertisements for a pharmaceutical company." Claire tapped away at the keyboard. "Let's see...secretary wanted. Must type 80 words per minute. That leaves me out." Claire spent the next hour browsing through job after job. She glumly realized she wasn't qualified for most positions in the history field. She had dropped out of her Master's program halfway through her second year when she landed the position at Gaston Pharmaceuticals thanks to a referral from an ex-boyfriend who used to work there. The money had been good and she had jumped at the opportunity. Now, she found herself with no job, a useless degree and no prospects. She closed her laptop and decided to call her mom.

"Hi, Mom! It's me, Claire," Claire said with a false cheerfulness.

"You're up bright and early on a Saturday. What's wrong?" Claire's mother, Mary, had a sixth sense when it came to her children.

"Well, let's see. I got laid off, found a kitten, and Darrin dumped me for a guy," Claire declared in a matter-of-fact tone. "Other than that, I'm good. And you?"

"Gracious! I didn't expect all of that. Let's back up. Start with losing your job," Mary said. Claire proceeded to tell her mother all that transpired the day before. When she finished, her mom was silent on the other end of the line.

"Mom, are you still there?" Claire asked.

"Sorry, dear. I was just thinking about what you said. The funniest thing happened the other day, and I haven't had a chance to talk to you about it. I received a letter from the law firm handling your Great Aunt Lily's estate. It's finally been settled and well, everything has been left to me. It's not much, but she left her farm and a small yearly allowance to operate it with the stipulation that it stay in the family. I would venture to say that you have no savings and now that Darrin is out of the picture, nothing to keep you in the city."

"I wouldn't say nothing. I have friends and a life and..." Claire trailed off as it dawned on her what her mother was suggesting. "Mom, are you suggesting I move to Aunt Lily's farm? In the country? With cows and things?"

"Why not? The house and farm needed to be sorted out and you could go for the short term while you figure out what you want to do. Expensive shoes and a nice wardrobe can only carry you so far in life. They certainly aren't going to pay your electric bill. Plus, you'd be helping me out. I don't have time to go up there to go through the house until the end of the school year. This is a win-win for you and me," Mary said emphatically. Claire's mother was an elementary school teacher, and she was used to having her directions followed. "Your father can't do it with his busy practice. Your sister is up to her eyeballs in wedding plans and your brother won't be back from Africa for at least three months. It makes sense."

"Let me think about it. I mean, everything just happened to me yesterday. I haven't even had time to sort it out in my brain or see if I can even get another job. Besides, the only time I've been to the country is the one time we visited Aunt Lily. I got stung by a bee and swelled up like a puffer fish. It wasn't exactly a good experience. Cows and chickens don't really hold any appeal for me." Claire shook her head at her mom's suggestion. Claire living in the country in her Ferragamo boots. It just wouldn't work.

"Well, don't think about it too long. Someone needs to head up and get the keys from the attorney's office and make sure the house is still standing. It's my understanding that a neighbor has been taking care of all of the animals and checking on the house. He's been kind enough to do it for the past two months, but I am sure he doesn't want to continue indefinitely. You could consider it a retreat. A chance to rethink the direction of your life. Regroup." Claire's father was a psychologist and unfortunately, his psychobabble worked his way into his wife's vocabulary.

"Give me a few days. I'll talk to you later, Mom. Love you," Claire said as she disconnected the call. Claire couldn't even wrap her brain around the idea of heading to the country. She was a city girl through and through. She loved the sounds and smells of the city streets. The bright lights and crowds were part of her. She couldn't even imagine not being able to get to a Starbucks in less than a few blocks.

Claire decided she needed a second opinion. She picked up her cell phone to call Isabella. "Isabella's House of Chaos. How can I be driven insane today?" Isabella answered. "Claire, I swear if these kids don't settle down I am going to lose my mind. We definitely need a spa day."

"Good morning to you, too. So, I'm not going to be Mrs. Stanislowski. In fact, no one will be Mrs. Stanislowski. It will end up being Dr. Darrin Stanislowski and Mr. Stanislowski," Claire gave a grimace as the image of Darrin slipping a diamond ring on another man's hairy knuckles formed in her mind.

"I don't get it. What the heck are you talking about?" Isabella demanded.

"Darrin needed to talk to me last night. He has decided to come out of the closet. I was the first person he came out to by dumping me for a guy. So I lost my job and my boyfriend to another man all in one day. This is what I get for cursing the universe. And now my mom wants me to go live on my Great Aunt Lily's farm and sort out her estate."

"Crap on a cracker! I knew something was off about that guy, but even I didn't see that one coming! I would love to have been a fly on the wall to see that meltdown. How badly did you hurt him?" Isabella asked.

"I didn't even raise my voice," Claire protested. "Well, okay, I did yell just a little, but can you blame me? I did not see this coming at all. I was a gay man's beard. I am a clueless idiot."

"You and the rest of us. Claire, I just thought he was uptight. I would never have guessed Darrin was gay. And your mom is crazy if she thinks you would survive in the country. She obviously didn't see you freak out when a pigeon came too close to you at the park. I thought you were going to hyperventilate and pass out from fear. A chicken would make you have a stroke," Isabella chuckled.

"I don't like pigeons. They are dirty birds. I could survive in the country if I had to. I just prefer the city. I haven't even had a day to look for a job. I'm sure I'll find something. If need be, I'll swing up to Cosner's Creek to make sure the farm is still standing then head back home," Claire said. She poured herself another cup of coffee and stirred the last bit of sugar she scraped from the sugar bowl. She would have to head to the store this morning to get groceries and some kitten food for Gingersnap.

"If you say so. Don't do anything rash. You've had a crappy twenty-four hours. I know you, chica, and you are going to do something crazy that you'll regret later. As your friend, I am telling you now - don't do it," Isabella warned.

"I'm not going to do anything crazy. Right now, I am going to head to the store. My kitten needs some food. Call me later," Claire said.

"Will do. Come by later today and I'll feed you. I'm making *chile rellenos* and flan just for you. Comfort food is a must in these trying times. Talk to you later." Isabella hung up. She knew the way to Claire's heart was through her cooking especially since Claire didn't cook. She microwaved. She tossed salads and occasionally made pasta but that was the extent of her kitchen skills.

Claire hopped in the shower. Once she toweled dry, she pulled on a sweatshirt she dug out of her messy dresser. She yanked a pair of yoga pants and socks out of her gym bag, sniffed them and deciding they could last at least another day, pulled them on. She put laundry on her to-do list for the day. Grabbing her keys, she walked down to the street and hopped into her Subaru. She turned the key and the engine roared to life. She put it into drive and as she pulled out, the car gave a horrible clunk, the check engine light came on, and it shuddered to a stop. Claire tried to start it again and nothing happened. Claire climbed out of the car and called the garage that did her oil changes and tune-ups. Twenty minutes later, a tow truck pulled up and Iggy hopped out. His dad owned the garage, but Iggy had taken over the day-to-day operations a year ago after his dad's heart attack.

"What's up, Miss O'Connor? O'Connor? Car won't

start?" Iggy chomped away at a piece of gum. His greasy black hair was styled into unbecoming spikes which gave him the look of a slightly crazed hedgehog. His face was pock-marked, and he had an unfortunately large beaked nose. His arms were covered with tattoos. If Claire hadn't known him for years, she would have crossed the street to avoid him, but he was actually a decent guy.

"I started to pull out and it gave a loud kerplunk. Then it died and wouldn't start back up," Claire shrugged her shoulders. "I don't know what's wrong with her." She handed Iggy her keys. He slid into the driver's seat and tried to start the car. Nothing happened. He hopped out and opened the hood. He fiddled with some wires and gave an occasional grunt. "How bad is it?"

"Well, it ain't good. I'm going to have to tow her to the shop. It looks like the timing belt and that is bad. It could be the death of this old girl." Iggy patted the hood of the car like it was an old horse.

"I can't afford a new car!" Claire wailed. "Heck, I can't afford this car if it's an expensive repair!"

"I'll see what I can do. I can't make you any promises. I'll call you later today and tell you the damage," Iggy said. "I won't charge you for the tow. It's just down the block anyway."

"Thanks, Iggy. Just do your best." Claire's shoulders slumped as she realized that her bad luck wasn't over. She headed down the street to walk to the market. It was only five blocks and the walk would clear her head. Obviously, someone was trying to tell her something. She had no job, no man, no money and now, no car. Her grandma said bad luck came in threes, so she was due some good luck. Maybe she should buy a lottery ticket. She kicked at a soda can in the middle of the sidewalk.

"Ma'am, there's no littering," A voice said from behind her. Startled, Claire turned and saw a policeman. He pulled out a book and a pen from his back pocket. "I'm going to have to write you a ticket."

"But...but...I...oh, never mind." Claire gave a dejected sigh and gave him her name and address. She snatched the ticket from his hand the second he reached out to hand it to her.

Claire walked the remaining few blocks to the market, picked up some kitten food and a few other essentials and headed home. When she opened her apartment door, Gingersnap ran up to greet her. "You know what, Ginger? I think the universe has been beating me over the head the past two days and telling me it is time to make a change. How about you and I take a little trip to the country?" Ginger meowed her agreement.

Claire turned her car turned down the lane marked with a large wooden sign that read "Lily Belle Farm." She had used the last of her savings to repair her car. Isabella had helped her pack her apartment and Claire's dad had hauled all of her furniture and dishes to a storage unit. Claire had brought her laptop, her clothes and a cat carrier with Ginger inside to Aunt Lily's farm. She wasn't planning on staying for more than two or three months, so she figured she wouldn't need too many things. She was doing what her mom suggested. Reevaluating her life and deciding what direction to go with her defunct career. She hadn't really liked writing ads. Her true passion was American history. Claire thought about returning to grad school and finishing her thesis. She could teach history at a local community college or get a job at a museum.

Her mind was wandering and she wasn't paying attention to the road in front of her. It wasn't until she heard a loud honk did she startle out of her reverie and realize that she had stopped her car. An old truck was behind her waiting for her to move. Pressing on the gas, Claire continued up the lane until she spotted Aunt Lily's farmhouse. It was much larger than she remembered. Pulling up to the house, she parked and stepped out to stretch her legs after the long drive. The driver of the old truck followed her into the driveway and pulled to a stop behind her car. A tall man stepped out and walked towards her.

"Can I help you?" The man asked as he squinted at Claire from under the brim of his battered cowboy hat. He wore a dusty pair of jeans with beat-up cowboy boots and his blue t-shirt stretched across his broad chest. Claire couldn't really see his face since it was hidden by the hat, but she didn't like the proprietary tone he took with her. This was her family's home and she had no clue who he was.

"I don't know. Can you?" Claire responded saucily. "This is my Great Aunt Lily's house. Well, it was her house. It's my mom's now. I'm Claire O'Connor. So the question is, who are you and how can I help you?"

"Whoa. A little prickly, aren't you. I'm Daniel Kirkpatrick. I've been taking care of your aunt's place since she passed away. I live right down the road at Hidden Acres Farm. I saw a strange car pulling up here and figured I'd better check it out. We don't get much crime in Cosner's Corner, but you never be too careful." Daniel took off the cowboy hat and Claire could see he had the brightest blue eyes she had ever seen. In fact, he was absolutely gorgeous. Curly black hair with tanned skin and a hint of an afternoon shadow on his chin. The chin even had a small cleft in the middle. He could have stepped out of *GQ* magazine. Claire gulped. Country life was already making her feel better.

"Sorry. I just drove four hours, got lost twice and haven't eaten since dawn. I'm a little on edge," Claire patted at her ponytail tucking the stray pieces behind her ear. She probably looked like a second-hand store reject after driving in the car with the windows rolled down. "It's nice to meet you. I appreciate you taking care of the farm until one of us could come up here."

"Not a problem. Did you already pick up keys to the place? The attorney said someone was coming up this week, so I put some milk in the fridge and there's a loaf of homemade bread in the breadbox. I cleaned out the refrigerator when Lily died, but the pantry is fully stocked with canned goods from last summer. You might need to light the stove though. It's kind of touchy, so if you'd like I can show you how to do it," Daniel offered.

"That would be great. I'm not much of a cook, so I'll probably just microwave something. Let me get my kitten out of the car." Claire reached in the car and grabbed Gingersnap's carrier.

"You won't be microwaving anything. This house hasn't been updated since the 1920s. It still has the old knob and tube wiring in place. There is no way a microwave would work in this old house. Haven't you ever been here before?" He grabbed the carrier from Claire as she fumbled with the set of keys the attorney had given her.

"I came here once as a child. My mom would come by herself to visit Aunt Lily. She said it was her break from her children to come to the country." Claire finally got the key to turn in the lock of the front door and it swung inward. "I'm not much of a country person. I've lived in the city my entire life. I had a chance to help my mom out by coming up here for a few months, so here I am."

She walked into the front entry of the house. Claire saw there were wide oak plank floors that were worn but had a warm glow from years of waxing. A large sitting room was off the hallway to the left. Claire took the cat carrier from Daniel and set it on the floor. When she opened the latch, a bright orange ball of fluff streaked out of the cage and darted under an armchair in the corner. Green eyes glared up at Claire. "Somebody's not happy riding in a car."

"Cute kitten. Your aunt has a cat. I took her back to my house since it didn't seem right to leave her here alone. Her name is Cream. She takes off and heads back here every chance she can slip out the door. If you don't mind, I'll bring her back here later today. Here, let me show you where everything is." Daniel walked out of the sitting room and back into the hallway. There was a stairway to the upstairs to the right of the front door, but Daniel headed down the hallway. The hall opened up into a dining room with a large oak table with four sturdy chairs around it. Heavy drapes hung over the windows shutting out the spring sun. Claire decided that she would have to let some light into the dark rooms. She had noticed that the sitting room had heavy drapes as well. Off the dining room was a large country kitchen. The cupboards had glass fronts and Claire spotted an eclectic mix of dishes. The counters were made of marble and wood which surprised Claire.

"The counters are beautiful! Is that really marble?" Claire trailed her fingers across the top of the cool surface.

"Yes. It's called a breadboard. This house was built in the twenties and was pretty modern for the time from what Lily said. The cook that used to live here with your aunt when she was young used to make pies and breads on that marble top. You're lucky that your aunt at least modernized the stove from coal to gas within the past fifty years. The old stove is out on the summer porch and Lily still used it for canning in the summer."

"I guess I'm going to have to learn to cook since I guess take-out isn't really an option around here," Claire joked. Her gaze took in the old refrigerator that looked like it had been here since the 1950s. A large sink with a hand pump caught her eye and she suddenly had a sinking thought. "Please tell me I have running water and an inside bathroom."

Daniel laughed. "You do. There is a small bathroom right behind that door over there and there is a full bathroom upstairs. The house has been updated some, but it still needs some work to bring it into the modern age."

"Well, I guess using my laptop is out of the question," Claire gave Daniel a wry smile. "I was going to try to update my resume and do some job hunting while I was up here, but that seems like it might be out of the question."

"You'll have to go to the coffee shop in Cosner's Corner if you want internet or to the local library. No Wi-Fi here. The goats don't really need it." Daniel opened up a door on the right side of the kitchen. "You've got a fully stocked pantry and this other door is the back stairway." He closed the pantry door and opened the door next to it. A set of stairs led upstairs.

Claire headed up the narrow stairs conscious of Daniel walking behind her. She was glad she had worn her Lucky jeans which gave her butt an extra boost. She came to the top of the stairs which opened to a large landing. Turning she walked down the hall and opened the first door to her left. Inside was a small, but neat bedroom with a single bed covered by a cheerful quilt. The next door opened up to a linen closet filled with sheets, towels and quilts. Claire opened the final door on the left and found what must have been her aunt's bedroom. A large bed was covered with a quilt made of varying shades of blue fabric. There was a large wooden wardrobe in the corner, a rocking chair and a bright rag rug on the wooden floor. Claire saw a faded pair of pink house slippers under the bed. It made her sad that she hadn't known her Great Aunt Lily. Claire and her sister preferred to visit their father's family who lived near the beach. Great Aunt Lily seemed eccentric living in her old farmhouse with her farm animals. Now Claire would never know what she was like and she realized a piece of her family's history had been lost with the death of her aunt.

Claire opened a door at the end of the hallway. It revealed a small bathroom with a large claw foot tub, a pedestal sink and thank goodness, a toilet. She noticed that there was no shower. Claire thought she might like sitting in the deep tub filled with bubbles. It really could be like a spa retreat.

"You'll like this next room," Daniel said as he led Claire back into the hallway. He opened the door on the right side of the hallway. Claire stepped into a room with a large window with a deep window seat perfect for sitting and reading a book. The room was painted a pale blue. There was a double bed on a white metal frame. A beautiful quilt of navy blue with applique stars covered the bed and a large handmade rug made from denim covered most of the hardwood floor. A bookcase stood against one wall and was filled with old books. A small white dresser sat in the corner.

"I love it. I'll move my things in here," Claire said decisively. She whirled around taking in the bright spring sunlight as it reached across the room. For the first time in a month, Claire felt a little glimmer of hope that her luck had changed. Maybe this country retreat would do her some good.

Daniel and Claire headed back downstairs using the front stairway. Gingersnap had ventured out from her hiding spot and was sniffing the doors and furniture.

"Let me go ahead and light the stove for you," Daniel offered as he headed back towards the kitchen.

As he worked on the stove, Claire opened the door off the back of the kitchen. She stepped out onto a large enclosed porch with a hammock and two rocking chairs. On the other end of the porch was the old coal stove with stacks of canning jars next to it. There were several pairs of boots lined up by the door. Claire gazed out into the backyard and spotted the large white barn surrounded by grassy fields.

"I've got the stove lit for you. It's time to feed the animals. You should come with me so you can see what to do." Daniel opened the screen door and headed towards the barn.

Reluctantly, Claire followed behind him. She had forgotten there were animals involved. She steeled her resolve. She could do this. How hard could it be? Throw some food in a bowl and give them water. Piece of cake.

"I've got this," Claire told herself. She stepped into the barn behind Daniel and the smell threatened to overwhelm her.

"Oh! What is that horrible smell?" Claire gagged.

Daniel laughed. "It's just Banjo. He's the male buck visiting Lily's does for the month. Lily had arranged for Joe Boxley to bring Banjo whenever Morning Dawn went into heat. I figured you would want to keep the same breeding schedule, so I went ahead and brought Banjo over."

"Buck? Doe? Heat? What the heck are you talking about?" Claire started to realize that she might be in over her head. "I thought Aunt Lily had a couple of cows and chickens and now you're talking about deer?"

"Deer?" Daniel let out a loud bark of laughter. "No, not deer. Come here and look." Daniel motioned for Claire to come look in the large pen at one side of the barn. She peered through the darkness to see a large white goat with long horns and a beard staring balefully at her. He stuck his nose into a hay feeder on the wall and pulled out a piece of hay and slowly chewed it. The musky odor was stronger near his pen.

"He needs a bath. He really stinks!" Claire shook her head.

"That's because male goats pee on their face to attract the females," Daniel told Claire with a grin. He leaned through the fence and patted the goat on his side.

"Now you're just yanking my chain. Really?" Claire gave him a look of disbelief. "If any guy I was interested in did that, I would run screaming in the other direction."

"I'm not kidding. We'll need to let him out into the pen with Morning Dawn tomorrow, but for now he can stay put. Come and meet the girls. We need to give them fresh hay and water. You give them grain in the morning, but not too much. They'll get fat."

Daniel led her out of the back of the barn and into the fenced field behind it. As they came back into the sunlight, a herd of white goats looked up from where they were nibbling on brush, then started trotting towards them. Claire let out a small scream of fright and hid behind Daniel.

"These are the does. They won't hurt you. The only thing they might do is nibble on your clothes," he said.

Claire stepped out from behind Daniel and timidly held out her hand to the goat closest to her. It leaned forward and nibbled on her fingers. Claire felt a little braver and she patted the goat on its head. "Nice goat. Pretty goat. Goat that doesn't want to eat me." Claire said in an effort to make friends. No sooner had she petted the one goat when others were butting their heads against her leg and vying for attention. "Whoa! One at a time!"

"They're hungry. Come here and I'll show you what to do." Daniel led her to a small door on one side of the door. Inside were bags with goat and chicken feed and buckets. Daniel showed her how much to feed them and how to fill the hay feeders. He showed her how much chicken feed to toss around the yard in the morning and afternoon and how to water all of them. Afterwards, Claire thought that it was definitely something she could handle.

"This isn't nearly as bad as I thought it would be," Claire said cheerfully to Daniel.

"Don't get too ahead of yourself. I'll be back in the

morning at six a.m. to show you how to milk the does that need it and then once a week you have to muck out the barn," Daniel instructed her.

"Milk? As in, milk coming from goats?" Claire gave Daniel an incredulous look. "Mucking?"

"You see that building over there?" Daniel pointed to a small building that Claire hadn't noticed before. A small stone path led between it and the house. "That is the milking shed and cheese house. Your aunt made goat cheese and sold it to the local restaurants in the area. She also sold it with her organic vegetables at the farmer's market in town on Saturday mornings. I assumed that whoever took over the farm was going to continue with the cheese and gardening."

"I don't know anything about cheese except that it tastes really good on a sandwich and I definitely don't know anything about gardening. What was my mother was thinking sending me up here to take care of this place? I should just get Gingersnap and head home." Claire gave a defected kick to the dirt in front of her. She noticed her designer boots had mud and muck from the barnyard on them. Great.

# ABOUT THE AUTHOR

Amy Lilly grew up in the small town of Cedaredge, Colorado where she spent her free time reading Nancy Drew mysteries and using her Junior Detective Kit to solve mysteries on her family farm. Amy earned a B.A. in English from the University of Iowa and her M.L.S. from SUNY at Buffalo. She spends her free time raising goats, chickens, a herd of well-fed cats and two hyperactive Jack Russell Terriers. She is married with two sons and two beautiful, smart granddaughters and lives in Virginia.

www.ingramcontent.com/pod-product-compliance
Lightning Source LLC
Chambersburg PA
CBHW070029120726
47909CB00003B/1102